To: Jasmine

What Ab

Never Stop Reading!

Enjoy Hinley's journey!
R. Jetleb
RJetleb

CAVERN
OF DREAMS
PUBLISHING

Publisher's Note: This is a work of fiction. Names, characters, places, and incidents are a product of the author's imagination.

Ordering Information:
Books may be ordered through Cavern of Dreams Publishing
43 Kerr-Shaver Terrace
Brantford, ON N3T 6H8
1-519-770-7515
(Discounts available for volume orders)

Published by
CAVERN OF DREAMS PUBLISHING
Brantford, Ontario, Canada

Library and Archives Canada Cataloguing in Publication

Jetleb, Regina, author
      What about Hailey? / written by Regina Jetleb ; edited by Bethany Jamieson, Danielle Tanguay, Mary M. Cushnie-Mansour.

Issued in print and electronic formats.
ISBN 978-1-927899-20-5 (paperback).--ISBN 978-1-927899-21-2 (pdf)

      I. Jamieson, Bethany, editor II. Tanguay, Danielle, editor
III. Cushnie-Mansour, Mary M., 1953-, editor IV. Title.

PS8619.E853W43 2016   C813'.6   C2015-907367-7
                                               C2015-907368-5

For Georgette, who got the ball rolling. Without her, this book would still be a manuscript, left sitting in a drawer, forgotten. Thanks for having such a loud mouth, dear sister-in-law!

Acknowledgements

To my husband and children, who had to forage, on many occasions, in the wilds of the kitchen for their own suppers while I tapped away furiously at the computer: writing, editing, rewriting, re-editing—thank you for your patience and understanding.

To Steph, my best friend, who eagerly read and critiqued all the drafts I sent her to her new home on the other side of the world, New Zealand. She tactfully pointed out errors or plot inconsistencies I had overlooked. I knew I could count on her, though, to temper her critique with generous amounts of sincere praise. Thank you, Steph! I owe my swelled head to you.

To K.S., who gets an honourable mention.

I would also like to acknowledge the fantastic editors at **Cavern of Dreams Publishing**. They cared for my manuscript as if it were their own! Bethany and Danielle, thank you both so much for helping me take my manuscript "to the next level!"

Chapter One

Hailey Williams sat back in her chair, crossed her arms over her chest, and looked around the table at her current foster family. They had just finished singing Happy Birthday to her. Hailey grimaced. *They wouldn't win any awards for that performance! Turning eleven is no big deal,* she thought as she flipped some of the bright pink ribbons that covered her birthday chair away from her T-shirt. Turning seven, now that had been a big deal. Her parents had still been alive then and not been in the car accident that had killed them instantly. Hailey had been in Mr. and Mrs. Dunlop's foster home for three months; however, Mrs. Dunlop's arthritis and Mr. Dunlop's heart problems were making it impossible for the Dunlops to continue fostering children for much longer. Two weeks ago, the Dunlops had explained to all the kids they would be looking for new homes for the foster children they now had. Hailey just hoped a permanent home would be found for her and her brother instead of another foster home.

"Blow out the candles, Hailey," begged her brother, Dylan, as he wiped his nose on his sleeve. Dylan was six years old and he could always make her laugh with his goofy faces and smile.

"Yeah, today would be nice," drawled twelve-year-old Keisha. She often had a sarcastic comment ready for her younger foster siblings.

Hailey rolled her eyes, leaned over the chocolate cake, and prepared to blow out the candles.

At that moment, Dylan sneezed all over his paper plate. Hailey jumped out of her chair, grabbed a Kleenex, and quickly wiped off Dylan's nose and felt his forehead. He didn't feel too warm, but she knew just how quickly a fever could come on. If Dylan's temperature spiked, it would bring on a seizure. She took a deep breath, made her wish, and blew out the candles.

"Cake, cake, we want cake!" hollered Dustin, Trevor, Taylor, and Keisha as they pounded their hands on the table.

Mrs. Dunlop looked on and gave a huge sigh. Hailey knew Mrs. Dunlop would run her fingers through her hair at any moment and moan about her foster children giving her yet another grey one. Hailey could feel her face go tight as she fought back tears. She didn't want to be in this foster home, and it made her sad Mrs. Dunlop seemed to see the foster kids, including Hailey, as nothing more than nuisances to be endured. Hailey grabbed the cake knife, waved it dramatically in the air and brought it down with a *plunk* onto the cake. The knife landed right in the neon blue icing that spelled "Best Wishes."

"Hey, what did you do that for?" whined eight-year-old Trevor. "Now you wrecked the cake."

"Yeah, we have to eat that thing too," chimed in nine-year-old Dustin.

Keisha tucked her curly brown hair behind her ear. "You messed up the icing. How do you expect me to eat that now?"

Hailey didn't care; the thought of getting older was making her lose her appetite. She was sure nobody would want to adopt an older child, let alone one who came with a younger brother. Everybody wanted babies. People were willing to wait years to adopt a cute, cuddly baby.

Mr. Dunlop smoothed back the five hairs he still had left on his head. "Troops, you need to settle down––no one has to eat cake if they don't want to."

Mrs. Dunlop picked up the knife Hailey had dropped on the table and served everyone a piece of cake.

Hailey picked at her cake. The other children, even Keisha, dove into their cake with enthusiasm. As she watched everyone eat, Hailey eyed the small stack of presents on the table. She really could use some new jeans or a new sweater, but the pile of presents looked too small to have any clothes in them. She looked down at her favourite jeans, now faded and with holes in the knees, and sighed. She could feel the metal button cutting into her waist. At least her blue T-shirt felt roomy and still looked relatively new.

"Open your presents now," demanded Taylor. Hailey looked over at Keisha and rolled her eyes. She was glad that, although Keisha might be rude sometimes, she had a friend at this foster home.

"Were we this impatient when we were in grade one?" Hailey asked Keisha.

Keisha nodded. "Oh yeah. I would have ripped all my presents open before even touching the cake."

"I've got better things to do with my time than sit here watching you take a century to unwrap some lousy gifts," said Dustin with a huge yawn as he ran his fingers over his newly spiked hair for the hundredth time that day.

"Yeah, me too," agreed Trevor as he slowly scraped the last of the icing off his plate with his finger. He seemed oblivious to the fact he could have scraped a pound of icing out of his short, black hair.

Hailey grabbed a present from the table and thought, *at least Dylan actually cares about celebrating my birthday.* She hated Dustin's and Trevor's lousy attitudes, and often worried Dylan would pick it up if he was in foster care long enough. She tore the wrapping off the first present: a plaid pencil case from Dustin. *Just what I need,* she thought, *a reminder school's starting in a couple of weeks.*

Hailey turned to Dustin. "Thanks for the pencil case." She choked back the sarcastic remark about him spending hours at the vending machine choosing her gift; she definitely did not want to behave like him in front of Dylan.

Keisha handed Hailey another present from the pile.

"Don't rip it!" yelled Taylor, as Hailey began tearing at the gift. "It's from Dylan and me."

As Hailey carefully pulled away the blue tissue paper, she could see why Taylor had yelled: the gift was two pictures drawn in crayon.

Taylor jumped down from the telephone book she sat on at the table, being careful to smooth down the yellow princess dress she always wore. She took the pictures out of Hailey's hand. "I'm going to explain them to you. Mine is a picture of the time Dylan and me were climbing the tree in the back, and Dylan fell down 'cause he was rolling his eyes."

Hailey remembered that day well. Dylan's seizure had lasted only a minute, but it had seemed like forever.

Taylor pushed her long, blond hair out of her eyes as she poked at the other picture. "This picture is from Dylan," she continued. "He can't draw too good because all he did was scribble." Taylor looked at Hailey and giggled. "You're touching dried-up snot. Dylan sneezed chunks all over the paper."

Mrs. Dunlop sighed and readjusted the pale-blue, silk scarf around her neck. "That wasn't very nice, Taylor. Remember now, children, if you can't say anything nice, then don't say anything at all."

Hailey groaned. That line was one they all heard daily. She looked over at her brother. He had just coughed and was wiping his nose on his favourite orange T-shirt again. She wished for the thousandth time he could be just like any other six-year-old, without any developmental delays or health issues at all. She and Dylan had been in five different foster homes. It seemed as if they moved every time Dylan had seizures. They just *had* to get adopted into a permanent home! Maybe this year her wish would come true.

Hailey unwrapped Trevor's gift next; it was Katy Perry's latest CD. "Thanks," she said. "I've wanted this for a while."

She began unwrapping the second-last gift from the pile. She could see from the label that it was from the Dunlops. She turned the gift around in her hands: it was a hardcover book with blank pages.

"If you don't feel comfortable talking about your feelings, maybe you can write them down instead," explained Mrs. Dunlop.

Hailey exhaled loudly. "Thanks a lot—I'm sure this journal will make a nice paperweight." She knew she was being rude, but what did it matter? Why should the Dunlops care if she got in touch with her feelings? Sooner or later, she and Dylan would be transferred from this home. It was less painful to feel angry than depressed.

Hailey took the last present off the table. It was from Keisha. She wasted no time tearing the wrapping off the gift. "All right!" she shrieked as she held the glossy, hardcover book on snowboarding in front of her.

"I found it at a garage sale a few weeks ago," said Keisha. "If you can't go snowboarding right now, at least you can look at the pictures and dream."

Hailey nodded. It would be totally amazing if she could learn to snowboard. She wanted to soar like a bird down the hills, the wind blowing all around her. She imagined snowboarding would feel like flying. The closest she had ever gotten to a snowboard, however, was when she had watched the Canadian snowboarder win the gold in the Winter Olympics.

Later that evening, after all the kids were in bed for the night, Hailey tossed and turned. It was another hot, August evening and her throat was very tight. It felt like there was hardly any room for air to get in and out of her lungs. Every breath was an effort. Hailey's asthma was as important as Dylan's seizures, but everyone seemed to forget that. She got out of bed to scrounge around in her bag for her blue inhaler; she needed a puff. She had been using inhalers since she was four and a half years old. One day, in the winter before she turned five, she had been running around her backyard, building snowmen, and having fun. Suddenly, she felt as if she couldn't breathe. She had never felt as terrified in her life as she did that day, trying to pull air into her lungs. She had gone to the hospital, where they gave her the medication she now needed to take every day. It helped her breathe normally almost immediately. Last year, as part of an independent study project, she had learned what asthma was. When her chest started to feel tight and she couldn't breathe well, it meant the breathing tubes in her lungs had gotten very narrow, not letting much air through. It was sort of like trying to breathe through a very thin straw. She also knew, from her own experience, cold air, running, and laughing could trigger an asthma attack. Her blue inhaler provided instant relief and Hailey made sure she always knew where it was.

As she rummaged, she became aware of Mr. Dunlop's deep voice. She could hear him well through the thin walls of the small house.

"How soon can the Marcottes visit Hailey and Dylan?" she heard Mr. Dunlop asking.

Hailey's heart stopped at his next statement. "Next week would be great. Mrs. Dunlop and I don't know how much longer we can care for them here."

Hailey didn't wait to hear more. She shoved her bag under her bed, took a quick puff of her inhaler, and hurried into the kitchen to ask Mr. Dunlop what was going on.

Chapter Two

Hailey walked into the kitchen to see Mr. Dunlop hanging up the phone.

"Who were you talking to?" she asked, her voice quivering slightly.

"I was talking to Anna. She has been in contact with a very nice family that would like to adopt you and Dylan."

"Why are you talking to our social worker so late?" demanded Hailey. "What's the big secret?"

Mr. Dunlop cleared his throat. "We didn't want to tell you about the Marcottes until we were absolutely sure they wanted to have a personal visit with just you. We didn't want you to get nervous or have any false hopes. David and Alexandra want to spend an afternoon with you next week."

"Wait, do you mean the David and Alexandra who are here, like, every other Sunday? I thought they were just your friends."

"They are, and they are also interested in adopting you."

Hailey had so many thoughts swirling around in her head that she couldn't respond for a minute. She had just about given up on the idea of being adopted. This seemed almost too good to be true. But why did the Marcottes want to adopt a moody, asthmatic eleven-year-old and a six-year-old who suffered frequent seizures and had developmental delays?

Hailey looked over at Mrs. Dunlop. She had just plugged the kettle in for a cup of tea. "Why would I get nervous? Dylan's seizures scared off the last family that wanted to adopt us. These people won't be any different."

"Oh no, dear, that's not the case at all," protested Mrs. Dunlop.

Hailey was just about to make it clear to Mrs. Dunlop that she did not want to be called "dear" when Dylan walked into the kitchen and wrapped himself around her leg. "I don't feel good," he moaned.

Hailey could feel how hot his little body was, draped around her bare leg. She disentangled herself from him. She could feel the sweat trickling down the back of her neck as she walked over to the sink, threw open the drawer beside it, and grabbed a cloth. Dylan had a fever and needed a cold cloth on his head immediately.

It was too late. Hailey turned from the sink just in time to catch Dylan as he slumped onto the kitchen floor. His eyes rolled back in his head and his body was twitching uncontrollably.

Hailey looked over at the Dunlops. Mrs. Dunlop was standing by the sink, wringing her hands. Mr. Dunlop headed toward the phone. This was Dylan's second seizure in this foster home and they still didn't know what to do.

"Run some cool water over the cloth and bring it to me," Hailey commanded. "I'll also need some medicine to give him after the seizure for his fever." Hailey carefully rolled Dylan onto his side so if he threw up he would not choke. She took the cloth from Mrs. Dunlop's shaking hand and put it on her brother's forehead.

"Emergency services are on the way," said Mr. Dunlop.

"A pillow would be nice!" Hailey barked. She hoped the Marcottes were better in a crisis than the Dunlops were.

Hailey used the pillow Mr. Dunlop handed her to cushion Dylan's head from the hard tile floor. "Maybe now you'll find time to renew your first aid," she snapped. On the day the Dunlops were going to renew their first aid certificates, Dustin had fallen off the climber in the backyard and needed stitches. The certificates had been forgotten in the excitement.

Mr. and Mrs. Dunlop nodded. Hailey stroked her brother's shaggy brown hair and waited for the seizure to run its course. Time seemed to stand still. It was so quiet in the kitchen, she could hear each second ticking by. She looked over at the large yellow clock again and again. With each second that went by, the ticking seemed to get louder.

Would the paramedics ever arrive? Every couple of seconds, Dylan's hand or leg would jerk with another convulsion. Just when Hailey was about to ask Mr. Dunlop to call 911 again, the paramedics knocked at the door. It was only when the two emergency technicians were in the house and examining Dylan that Hailey felt she could breathe freely again.

"Is my brother going to be okay?" asked Hailey.

"He's going to be fine," responded the slim paramedic. She stood up from Dylan's side. "You his sister?"

"Yeah. You sure he's alright now?" Hailey persisted. She wasn't in the mood for small talk.

"Yes, he'll be good as new now," said the slim paramedic's partner. "You handled his seizure very well."

Hailey didn't answer. Three years on her own with Dylan had given her a lot of experience in dealing with his seizures.

The paramedics left and Hailey brushed off Mr. and Mrs. Dunlop's attempts to help put Dylan to bed. "Just let me give him his medicine and get him into bed—you can go off and make more secret plans or something." She was being rude again, but it didn't matter. They were leaving.

Hailey crawled into Dylan's small bed with him and rubbed his back. He had taken his medicine and was now curled up, fast asleep. She allowed herself the luxury of a long, drawn-out sigh. It had been a long day. She wondered what the Marcottes were really like. She wished she had paid more attention when they visited. Why were they interested in her and Dylan anyway? What had the Dunlops told them about Dylan's seizures? She remembered something her mother had been fond of saying: "Families stay together through good times and bad, through thick and thin." Well, this was definitely one of the bad times. Would the

Marcottes be the kind of people who gave up on kids when the going got tough? What if they were just like all the other foster parents, quick to unload children with medical problems?

Hailey felt Dylan's head one more time to make sure he was really okay. His seizures had always scared her. Would the Marcottes really want to adopt two children with major medical problems? This was only the second time in three years that anyone had been interested in adopting both Dylan and Hailey and keeping them together.

Hailey carefully got out of Dylan's bed and readjusted his covers. She couldn't stop worrying about the Marcottes—they just had to adopt her and Dylan! Time was running out; Hailey wasn't getting any younger, or cuter.

Hailey tiptoed out of Dylan's room and quietly opened the door to the room she shared with Keisha. She knew the Marcottes would have enough to deal with handling Dylan's seizures; she would have to make sure the Marcottes didn't see her use her inhaler. If she acted like her asthma was no big deal, they might have a better chance of being adopted.

Hailey sighed and got into bed. It was a long time before she was able to fall asleep.

Chapter Three

The following Wednesday, Hailey woke up early. She was trying to make the most of the time she had left to sleep in before school started again, and waking up early was frustrating. Why couldn't she sleep in?

"Time to wake up," came Mrs. Dunlop's voice at the door. "It's a big day for you and Dylan."

Now Hailey knew why her throat felt dry and she couldn't swallow: today she and Dylan were going to spend the day with the Marcottes.

Hailey rolled over in her bed. "I'm up already. Go wake someone else up," she croaked.

At breakfast, Hailey could only eat a few bites of her oatmeal. Dylan hardly ate anything either, but that was because he was so excited he kept jumping out of his chair and running to the door every time he thought he heard a car in the driveway.

Finally, after Dylan had made his fifth trip to the front door, Hailey resorted to bribing him to finish his breakfast. "Eat your cereal and I'll show you how to make a really cool paper airplane," she promised. Dylan hopped onto his chair and began spooning Cheerios into his mouth.

After breakfast, and making Dylan's paper airplane, Hailey and Dylan headed into the backyard. She sat on the swing and watched as Dylan circled around, arms outstretched, pretending he was an airplane. Hailey hoped the Marcottes really did want to adopt them. She knew if she and Dylan made a good impression, the Marcottes would be more likely to choose them. She reminded herself to watch her temper—she didn't want to say things she'd later regret.

Hailey was so lost in thought, she jumped when Keisha grabbed one of the chains of the swing she was sitting on. "Do you want to go to the store for a snack?" asked Keisha.

"No, the Marcottes are taking us out for burgers," answered Hailey. "I don't want to be too full to enjoy burgers Mr. Dunlop didn't burn."

"Okay, see you later," said Keisha as she headed out of the backyard, jingling the coins in her pocket.

"They're here, they're here!" screeched Dylan, still flapping his arms and pretending he was a plane. "Vroom, vroom, the airplane is flying over to see them!"

Hailey looked up. She could see David and Alexandra getting out of their car. Dylan ran toward them, but she didn't follow; she took several deep breaths to calm the butterflies in her stomach. Hailey knew, at any moment, Mr. Dunlop would bring the Marcottes into the backyard. After what seemed like forever, she saw Mr. Dunlop emerge from the house and lead the Marcottes over, Dylan skipping along behind them.

"Hi Hailey," said Alexandra, looking at her with kind, blue eyes. Dylan pressed his sticky little hand into Hailey's. She squeezed it reassuringly. Dylan was nervous too.

Hailey glanced at the couple standing in front of her. Alexandra was wearing a blue, plaid shirt over a white tank top and jeans. David was very tall and thin. He was wearing khaki shorts and a green T-shirt. They were both smiling, and not in that forced way Hailey noticed some adults did when they felt uncomfortable.

Hailey was tongue-tied. She managed a weak, "Hi."

Alexandra ran a hand through her wavy brown hair. "I'm sure we'll find more to talk about when we get to know each other better, Hailey."

Alexandra knelt down in front of Dylan. "I'm looking forward to spending the afternoon with you Dylan," she said.

David adjusted his frameless glasses and ran his fingers through his short black hair. "You ready to go?" he asked. "I thought we could eat at a restaurant near the airport. I heard Dylan likes planes."

Dylan immediately let go of Hailey's hand. "Let's see airplanes!"

He grabbed David's hand and started pulling him out of the backyard.

Hailey got off the swing and followed Dylan, David, and Alexandra. Dylan eagerly got into the back of their green station wagon and proceeded to push all the window and door locks.

"Dylan, don't push those buttons. It could be dangerous for you," said Hailey as she clipped Dylan's seatbelt around him.

Alexandra turned to Hailey. "Do you need some help with your seatbelt?" she asked.

"No thank you. I think I mastered seatbelts in kindergarten," snapped Hailey, instantly regretting it. She shook her head in annoyance. There was no need to snap at the Marcottes, they didn't know everything about her and Dylan, just like she didn't know a lot of details about them. She needed to cut them some slack and curb her rude comments.

"Great! Then we're all set to leave." Alexandra smiled at Hailey.

Hailey clicked her seatbelt on as hard and as loud as she could. Making a good first impression didn't need to be so hard, did it? She let out a huge sigh and leaned back against the seat.

"Our wagon is roomy; there'll be lots of space for you in the back, Anna," said David, as he opened the car door. Hailey had forgotten their social worker was coming along for their first meeting. Anna was the world's biggest blabbermouth. She loved toting around her brown briefcase and consulting her notes. Hailey knew that after consulting those top-secret notes, Anna would have lots to tell the Marcottes about Hailey and Dylan. She couldn't stop another huge sigh from escaping.

"Are you feeling ill, dear?" asked Anna as she clasped Hailey's hand.

Hailey pulled her hot hand out from under Anna's cool one. "No, I'm just dandy," she answered sarcastically.

"Hailey's probably feeling a bit nervous," whispered Anna loudly. She leaned toward David and Alexandra. "That reminds me, did I tell you about Hailey's breathing difficulties?"

"It's called asthma, for your information," interjected Hailey, "you can call it what it is." She wished Anna wouldn't whisper like that right in front of her, as if she weren't even there.

Dylan was fiddling with the buttons again. Hailey gently took his hand and looked carefully at him. "Don't touch Dyl—danger," she reminded him.

David glanced in the rear view mirror at Hailey. "All the buttons in the back have child safety locks, which we control in the front. Did you notice nothing happens when Dylan pushes the buttons?"

Hailey had not noticed, but she nodded her head at David anyway. When was the ride going to end?

They arrived at the fast food restaurant about fifteen minutes later. Hailey had to hold Dylan's hand tightly to keep him from jumping around in the parking lot.

"Planes, planes, planes! Look at the planes!" shouted Dylan as he craned his neck to watch the tarmac beside the restaurant. There were a lot of planes. It seemed like one came and went every minute, and they were so close it felt as if you could reach out and touch them.

Dylan was the first to see all the picnic benches outside. "Let's eat outside! Pleeease?" he asked.

Alexandra knelt down and gave him a big hug. "I think it would be a lovely idea to eat outside," she said.

Dylan shrieked with delight.

Hailey shuddered inside. How could Alexandra hug him like that on the first day? She hardly knew him!

When they were all seated at a picnic table with their order, Alexandra turned to Hailey and Dylan. "I know this must be an awkward time for you, but I'm hoping we can get to know each other just a little bit today."

Hailey stared down at her hamburger. "You need to talk to Dylan in short sentences; otherwise, he doesn't understand what you're saying," she mumbled.

"Thank you for letting me know that," answered Alexandra. "You've had quite a lot of experience looking after your little brother, haven't you?"

"I guess so; I've lived with him for six years now."

Hailey had to keep grabbing Dylan's hand to keep him from jumping off the bench and running after the squirrels he saw. As she encouraged him to keep eating, she listened to Anna talking with David and Alexandra.

"Dylan has some minor developmental delays as a result of his many seizures," said Anna, consulting her notes.

"No, he just learns differently than most kids, and he only sometimes has seizures," interrupted Hailey.

Anna nodded. "You're right. I'm sorry if I'm describing your brother differently than you would."

Alexandra finished chewing one of her fries and looked at Hailey. "How would you describe Dylan? How would you describe yourself?" she asked.

Hailey had never been asked to describe herself or Dylan. What was she supposed to say? To avoid answering, she quickly took a giant bite out of her burger. Mayonnaise oozed out of the burger and onto her blue T-shirt. She looked around on the table for napkins. They must have forgotten to pick some up. She quickly wiped off her mouth and her shirt with her hand.

David handed Hailey a napkin, which had slipped from view under the fry container. "Here, try one of these. They work really well," he joked.

"You were going to describe yourself and your brother to the Marcottes," Anna reminded her.

~ 23 ~

Hailey had been hoping they would forget. She could feel her face getting hot. Why couldn't Anna just drop the issue? She certainly had a way of making Hailey's temper rise! Hailey didn't want to be sitting there and answering questions about herself. Hailey didn't want to have to look for a family. She wanted the one she and Dylan had had. Having Anna around reminded her that her parents were dead, and her presence agitated Hailey to the point she struggled to control her attitude. She knew she was wrecking the whole afternoon. It would be better if she just made herself scarce and left Dylan to charm them.

Hailey made her answer as short and as vague as possible. "Dylan likes everybody and it's easy to make him smile. I just turned eleven and I'm choosy about who I like and don't like." She got up from the bench. "Are we done yet?"

"Well, no, not yet. The Marcottes have brought along a special family album they made so you could see their house and the neighbourhood they live in," Anna said. "Sit down for five more minutes."

Hailey plunked herself down on the bench. Dylan eagerly turned the pages in the book, looking at all the photos. Hailey glanced over occasionally. From what she could see, the Marcottes lived in an average-looking house on an average-looking street.

"What's your favourite subject in school?" David asked Hailey.

Hailey was hot and tired and not in the mood to answer any more questions. "Lunch," she said as she took one last sip of her drink. She immediately felt ashamed of her rude comment.

She was sure she saw David and Alexandra exchange a this-kid-is-a-pain look. Hailey squashed her cup flat on the table as she thought about how she could backtrack and make up for her snippy remarks this afternoon.

Suddenly, Dylan took off like a rocket toward a squirrel he saw. He headed right for the busy parking lot, and didn't see the white van headed right for him!

Chapter Four

"Dylan! Stop!" shouted Hailey as loudly as she could. She took off after him, but Dylan kept running. She screamed again. Finally, the van driver heard Hailey's desperate shout. He noticed Dylan, slammed on the brakes, and steered around him—right into some large recycling bins.

Hailey grabbed Dylan and pulled him over to the side of the parking lot. "What did you do that for? Didn't you see the van? Didn't you?" she shouted.

David and Alexandra came running over. "Deep breaths, Hailey," David instructed. "Everything's okay now."

Dylan started to cry. "I'm sorry, I chasing a squirrel," he sobbed.

Hailey reached into her pocket, pulled out a tissue, and gently wiped Dylan's tears. "I'm sorry Dylan, you just scared me so much," she explained. "I thought the van was going to hit you."

Dylan started to smile. "You not angry with me?" he said, wiping the tears from his face.

"No, I'm just glad you're okay," Hailey answered. She wrapped her arms around her little brother and gave him a big squeeze.

When Hailey finally let him go, Alexandra hugged Dylan for a long moment as well.

"Do you need help picking up those papers, lady?" asked the van driver. Hailey looked over and saw Anna frantically picking up the contents of her briefcase, which were spread everywhere across the parking lot.

Anna straightened her flower-print skirt. "No, I'm alright, thanks," she answered the grubby-looking driver, "I just need to find my heel."

Hailey smirked as she realized what had happened. Anna had also been running to stop Dylan, and her ridiculously high heels had tripped her up and she had gone sprawling.

David chased down the last of Anna's papers and handed them to her.

"Motor oil is a good look for you," Hailey murmured to herself, as she tried to concentrate on slowing her breathing. Thank goodness she had brought her inhaler. She tried not to stare at the huge oil stain on Anna's skirt as she thought about when would be the best time to take her puffer. Almost every time she ran she needed to use it, but she still thought it would be better if the Marcottes didn't see her use her inhaler on the first visit. She and Dylan had already made enough of a bad impression. Hailey hoped they still had a chance of being adopted. Hailey lagged behind as they headed to the car and quickly took a puff of her inhaler when she thought nobody was looking.

When they arrived back at the Dunlops, Hailey turned to David and Alexandra as soon as she and Dylan got out of their car. She swallowed hard. "I'm sorry for being rude at lunch."

"That's okay," replied David reassuringly. "I think we were all a bit nervous today."

Hailey let out a breath she didn't even know she'd been holding. Making that apology was easier than she thought it would be; David didn't seem nearly as angry about her rude attitude as she had imagined.

Later that evening, Keisha and Hailey sat on the porch drinking juice. As Hailey described Anna chasing her papers around the parking lot, Keisha laughed so hard purple juice came squirting out her nose. When Keisha finally managed to tame the laughter down to giggles, she shook her head. "Grownups are too strange sometimes, aren't they?" she snickered.

Hailey laughed. "Yeah, we should charge admission just to watch them go about their daily lives. Oh, and guess what?"

"Chicken butt," responded Keisha with a huge grin.

"Seriously. You'll never guess what David and Alexandra told us on the way home," said Hailey as she put down her juice glass.

"They told you they're actually aliens and they're going to take you with them on their spaceship where they do experiments on deranged kids like you and Dylan?" joked Keisha.

"If I'm deranged, then you are totally mental," laughed Hailey.

"So tell me already what the big deal is," demanded Keisha. She leaned back on the porch swing.

"Every Christmas they take a four-day downhill skiing and snowboarding trip!" exclaimed Hailey.

Keisha leaned forward. "Cool! If they adopt you, you'll go with them and you could actually learn to snowboard! But, won't you need more than four days to learn how to recognize a snowboard?"

"Thanks for your support, headcase!" growled Hailey as she punched Keisha's arm.

On Friday, Hailey packed for their first weekend visit with the Marcottes. She had already checked and rechecked to make sure Dylan's medicine was in the bag; he had another ear infection. She tossed her inhalers into the duffel bag as she thought about the weekend ahead. Even though she hated having a social worker, the reality was that she needed Anna to help her and her brother find their forever family. If she couldn't have her own family back, the Marcottes seemed like they could be that forever family. It was still hard for her, though, to accept her parents were gone. Sometimes she liked to pretend they were simply on an extended vacation and would be back any day to pick her and Dylan up. But, she had readily agreed to a weekend visit with the Marcottes when Anna had asked her; she had been surprised and relieved the Marcottes still wanted to have them over for the weekend after their disastrous meeting.

She lay back on her bed and sternly told herself not to feel anxious. Making a good impression and not saying the wrong thing was turning out to be harder than she thought, and now, because she was afraid of saying or doing the wrong thing, she was freaking out about spending the weekend with perfectly ordinary adults.

Hailey got up off the bed. She needed a plan. Plans of action always helped her to feel better—they gave her something to do instead of just feeling nervous. She paced the room as she thought. What if she just relaxed and didn't worry so much about making a good impression? Then, if the Marcottes still chose to adopt her in spite of her less-than-perfect behaviour, everything would work out. *Yeah, that sounds good!* Hailey smiled. It would show her if the Marcottes could stick with her through thick and thin.

Dylan burst into the room. "They're here, Hailey! Come on, let's go," he urged.

"I'm coming," answered Hailey. It felt like a ten-pound weight had been lifted off her shoulders. She would just concentrate on having a good time and not worry too much about behaving perfectly.

Dylan pulled Hailey out of the room so quickly she barely had time to pick up her overnight bag.

The ride to the Marcotte's house took about forty minutes. Dylan spent the entire time looking at the photo of their house and comparing it to houses he saw along the way. "No, not that one. No, not that one too," he kept saying.

When they arrived, David gave Hailey and Dylan a tour of the house. They would each have their own room! Hailey crammed all her things into the top drawer of her dresser. She looked briefly at her red inhaler—the label still looked new. She thought about what the doctor had told her: she was supposed to take that inhaler every day to prevent asthma attacks; the medicine was supposed to keep the breathing tubes in her lungs from swelling closed. But Hailey had only taken the red inhaler three or four times in the last year, it was such a nuisance to take every day! She had to wait one minute between puffs and rinse her mouth with water afterwards. Who had time for that? Besides, it didn't seem to make much difference in preventing asthma attacks anyway. She left the inhaler lying on her nightstand and went into Dylan's room, unpacked his bag, and stuck his medication into her pocket.

Hailey wandered through the living room to the kitchen where she could hear Dylan happily chattering. Alexandra was baking cookies with him.

"Come on in, we can always use more bakers," Alexandra said as she spooned some dough onto a cookie sheet.

"No, I'd rather eat cookies than make them," answered Hailey. "I need to put Dylan's antibiotic in the fridge. He gets it at 8 o'clock sharp. I'm the only one he'll take medicine from."

Alexandra gestured in the direction of the refrigerator. "You can put it anywhere there's room."

Hailey put the medicine in the fridge and watched suspiciously as Dylan dug right in and started putting cookie dough on the sheet. "Look at me, Hailey. I baking cookies," Dylan said, licking his fingers.

Hailey couldn't return her brother's wide smile. Why was everything so easy for him? How did he know the Marcottes weren't going to let him down?

Hailey turned and stomped out of the room toward her bedroom. Each stomp on the hardwood floor helped her to stem the tears that had already started down her cheeks. She used to love baking with her mother; it had been one of their favourite activities to do together. Hailey threw herself down on the bed, picked up her used portable CD player, and turned on the tunes. The relentless beat helped keep the sad thoughts from settling in her head.

At dinner that evening, Hailey focused on helping Dylan eat his spaghetti. "The noodles are too long, he can't eat stuff like this," she said as she took minuscule forkfuls of her own meal.

"You need to eat more than that, Hailey. You're going to be hungry later this evening," warned Alexandra.

"I'm going to throw this stuff up if I eat anymore," grumbled Hailey.

"Suit yourself," answered David. "The kitchen closes after dinner—no special requests later if you choose not to eat now."

Hailey twirled a strand of spaghetti around her fork. She wondered if this was some kind of tough love. At the Dunlops', the kitchen was never closed. She didn't remember her parents ever talking to her like that either. Hailey managed to finish her dinner; Alexandra had not loaded up her plate the way Mrs. Dunlop always did.

After dinner, Hailey gave Dylan his bath and made sure he got his medicine on his special magic spoon. "Here comes the magic spoon, Dylan," she sang. She zoomed the spoon around, making airplane noises as she brought the spoon to his mouth. Dylan grinned and eagerly opened his mouth so the "airplane" could fly in.

A few minutes later, she tucked Dylan into bed. Alexandra and David hovered in the doorway.

"What is it?" asked Hailey, frowning.

"We'd like to say good night to Dylan, as well," replied Alexandra. She had her hands tucked into the front pockets of her jeans.

Hailey was just about to tell them Dylan didn't like strangers tucking him into bed when Dylan hopped out of bed and wrapped himself around David. "Good night David and good night 'Andra," he chirped. "Can we see planes again tomorrow?"

David and Alexandra looked at each other and smiled. "Tomorrow we're going to Centre Island; maybe there you'll see some planes in the sky," said David.

That was just what Dylan wanted to hear. He would go to sleep dreaming of planes.

Later, Hailey got into bed and read her book until she could barely keep her eyes open. When Alexandra and David wished her good night, she mumbled "Night," down into her book.

That night, Hailey dreamt of huge, people-sized cookies chasing her around the house, saying they had already eaten her brother and he was delicious. Hailey woke up with a start. She was in a sweat and breathing heavily.

Alexandra came into her room and put on the night-light. "Are you okay?" she asked. "I heard you groaning. Do you need to take your inhaler?"

Hailey brushed Alexandra off. "I'm fine. I'm going back to sleep now," she answered. But as soon as Alexandra left the room, Hailey reached for her inhaler, took a puff, then lay back down, her heart still pounding. Could she survive the rest of the weekend with the Marcottes?

Chapter Five

Dylan's voice was the first thing Hailey heard when she woke up the next morning. He was asking something about putting blueberries in pancakes. Hailey lay in bed for a moment as it slowly came to her that she was still at the Marcottes'. She got out of bed and yawned hugely. Even though it had taken forever to fall asleep, the soft sheets and comfortable pillow had helped her to feel rested. Her breathing seemed funny though. Just one quick puff of her inhaler and she knew she would be ready to face the day.

Hailey took a minute to really look around her new room. In the sunlight, everything looked brighter than it had yesterday. As she walked over to the closet, she imagined what it would be like to find a brand new snowboard nestled in among her clothes. Playing imagination games was something she had started doing shortly after living in her first foster home; it helped her to pass the time and cope with situations she didn't like being in. Hailey swung the closet door open with a wide sweep of her arm. Her mouth hung open as she looked at two new outfits in the closet. What was this? Where had they come from? As she headed out of her room to find out about the clothes, Alexandra walked in.

"Good morning. I see you found the clothes. I hope you don't mind, we thought you could use some new jeans and shirts," said Alexandra.

Hailey was quite touched the Marcottes had noticed she needed some new clothes, but she couldn't stop her rude response. "Do my brother and I look poor and ragged or something? We don't need your charity, you know."

Alexandra crossed her arms over her chest. "Your rude attitude is wearing very thin with me," she reprimanded Hailey. "Anna let us know you were growing out of the clothes you have now, so David and I thought we would surprise you. If you don't like surprises, or if you don't appreciate us choosing clothes for you, then all you need to do is tell us, politely and respectfully. I'm going to leave and close your door. When I open it again, you're going to have a second chance to begin your day in a more positive mood."

Alexandra walked out, firmly shutting the bedroom door.

Hailey threw herself down on the bed. There was no doubt she deserved that. She didn't like to see Alexandra's eyes flashing so angrily, and she was surprised how awful and afraid she felt. She didn't want her plan to work so well that she blew her chance of getting adopted! Hailey buried her face in the pillow to keep the tears from starting.

Alexandra opened the door. "Good morning, Hailey," she said. "Breakfast will be ready in about five minutes. Please be sure you wash your face and comb your hair before you come to the table." She closed the door again.

Hailey slowly sat up, walked to the closet, and pulled a pair of white, jean short overalls off the hanger, then rummaged through her bag until she found a yellow shirt to go with them. She went to the bathroom where she quickly ran a comb through her hair and dragged a damp washcloth across her face before she made her way into the kitchen.

Hailey's heart melted when she saw Dylan wearing an oversized chef's hat as he stirred something in a large bowl. He was also wearing jean short overalls and a yellow shirt.

David turned and winked at Hailey. "Wow, you two must have a psychic sibling connection," he laughed.

Hailey couldn't help but smile. It was cool she and Dylan were wearing the same outfit.

David held out a spoon laden with batter. "Here, taste our secret blueberry mixture," he offered.

"It's going to drip on the floor, David," warned Alexandra, brushing flour off her jeans.

Hailey took a cautious lick of the spoon. The batter tasted pretty good.

Hailey went over to Dylan and gave him a hug.

"Did you sleep well, Dyl?" she asked, quickly touching his forehead to make sure he wasn't getting a fever.

Dylan nodded. "I slept real good. I have airplane sheets."

Hailey looked over at David cleaning up the batter that had landed on the floor. "He means his sheets and pillowcase have pictures of airplanes on them," explained David.

Hailey nodded and sat down at the table, not daring to look at Alexandra. Was she still angry? Were she and David going to change their minds and not adopt them after all? Or, maybe, they would just take Dylan?

She quickly wiped her sweaty palms on her overalls and took a deep breath. "I'm sorry I was rude this morning," she said. She felt as if she had just swallowed some chalk.

Alexandra sat down opposite Hailey at the table and touched her hand. "Your apology means a great deal to me. Thank you."

Hailey picked up her fork and knife to help Dylan cut up his pancakes. She was glad Alexandra had accepted her apology.

After breakfast, once Hailey and Dylan had each eaten half a dozen pancakes washed down with orange juice, David reminded them about the trip to Centre Island. Dylan jumped up and down and grabbed Hailey's overall strap. "We love Centre Island," he said. He looked up at Hailey. "'Member the super magic maze?"

Alexandra smiled. "I'm glad you like the island. The ferry ride over will be fun too," she said.

"Come on, Dylan," urged Hailey. "I need to sunscreen you so big, bad, old Mr. Sun doesn't burn you." Hailey led Dylan into her room and began covering him with the protective lotion. "Stop wiggling, you little monster, or we'll never get to the island," scolded Hailey. She wasn't really angry with Dylan. Who could be?

"Do you need some help?" asked Alexandra.

"No, we've got this," answered Hailey. She didn't look up at Alexandra in the doorway.

"Don't forget your hat," Hailey reminded Dylan. She made herself busy packing a small bag with her inhalers, the sunscreen, a change of clothes for Dylan, and a water bottle. When the bag was packed the way she liked, she looked up and saw Alexandra was no longer in the doorway.

Hailey took the bag into the kitchen. "Could I get some ice cubes for this water bottle?" she asked.

"That's a good idea," responded David, as he took the water bottle from Hailey. "Would you like us to pack your things in our bag?"

"No," replied Hailey, "like I said to Alexandra, we've got this under control."

Hailey made sure she held Dylan's hand tightly when they got to the ferry. He wanted to run all over, trying to see everything at once. The last thing she needed was for him to get lost.

As she leaned over the railing on the top level of the ferry, Hailey wished she had worn her sunglasses. She had found them for a dollar at a garage sale; they were not designer shades, but, at least, they would have kept the sun out of her eyes. She shut her eyes instead and enjoyed feeling the soft spray of water splashing on the side of the ferry as it made its way across the harbour. Every once in a while, she glanced over at David and Alexandra. Alexandra had brought along a sketchbook, and from what Hailey could see, she was busy drawing the many sailboats floating around the Toronto Harbour. David was sitting back beside Alexandra, his fingers laced behind his head.

When they arrived at the island, Dylan insisted on going to the super magic maze. "Please, please, Hailey and me, we wanna go to the maze!"

David swung Dylan up onto his shoulders. "Let's go then! I'm curious about this maze," replied David.

Alexandra followed behind David and Dylan, but Hailey lingered behind, walking slowly. She remembered the last time she had been in the maze; she and Dylan had spent the entire morning in the maze with their mother. That had been a wonderful day. Hailey had laughed so much she had thrown up. Hailey's throwing up had made them laugh even harder.

When they finally reached the maze, made entirely of tall, leafy hedges, Hailey sat on one of the large boulders at the entrance. Her throat felt tight. She concentrated on studying the ground beneath her feet. Suddenly Dylan grabbed her hand and tried to pull her to her feet. "Come in the maze with me, Hailey," he pleaded.

"Dylan, why don't you show David around the maze so he doesn't get lost?" intervened Alexandra.

Dylan let go of Hailey's hand and ran over to David. "Come on! Let's go have fun," he said, taking David's hand as easily as he had Hailey's.

"I guess this place holds fond memories for you," said Alexandra as she sat down beside Hailey. Hailey could only nod in response. They sat in silence. Sitting together quietly with Alexandra was something she had often done with her mother. Hailey shut her eyes, enjoying the moment, and pretended she was really Alexandra's daughter. Occasionally Hailey could hear Dylan's familiar shrieks of delight. When David and Dylan re-emerged from the maze, they were both flushed and laughing.

Dylan easily filled the silence with his noisy chatter.

"I fell down and got a scrape on my knee. David says I'm tough, but I need a Band-Aid."

"Let me see," replied Alexandra as she fished in her large straw bag.

"How about a picnic lunch after we patch Dylan's knee?" asked David. Hailey shrugged. She was more thirsty than hungry at that moment.

Dylan sat down on the grass. "Let's eat here," he insisted. "It's nice."

"I know a beautiful place by the lake where we can eat in the shade," suggested Alexandra. She helped Dylan to his feet. "Did you know there's an airport on this island, Dylan?"

Hailey kicked a stone. This was the first time she and Dylan had been at the Island since their parents died. She loved it here, but the great memories she had were painful to relive. To keep from feeling sad, she snipped at Alexandra angrily. "Of course he knows about the airport."

Talk of the airport was enough to distract Dylan, and they all headed toward the picnic spot. David and Alexandra had packed a picnic lunch complete with sandwiches, sliced apples, juice, and cookies. Dylan ate very little. He busied himself feeding the pigeons or running at them and laughing as they scattered. Hailey nibbled at one peanut butter and banana sandwich and filled up on the peach punch. It was really delicious. She didn't feel like eating the homemade chocolate chip cookies, though. She could still taste the chocolate chip cookies she and her mom used to make, she didn't want to eat Alexandra's. They were sure to be different and she wanted to remember only the taste of her mother's cookies. It seemed silly, holding on to the taste of chocolate chip cookies as a way of remembering someone, but it was comforting to Hailey.

"Hey, who's up for a round of mini-golf?" suggested Alexandra after lunch.

Again, Hailey shrugged. She was curious to try it out, but she had never actually played. She felt embarrassed about admitting it to the Marcottes.

"We'll be glad to give you some pointers. Playing mini-golf is how David and I met." Alexandra looked over at her husband and smiled.

Hailey enjoyed the game. Using the putter to guide the ball into the small holes wasn't as hard as she had thought. It was a good challenge. David kept Dylan out of Hailey's way so she could have a clear shot at every hole. It was relaxing not to have to keep such a watchful eye out for her overactive brother.

After their mini-golf game, they went on several rides, including the mini rollercoaster, the old-fashioned cars, and the Sky Ride. Hailey loved the Sky Ride. She had been too afraid to go on it the last time she had been here, but now it was a blast.

Dylan didn't want to go on the log ride, so David and Hailey went on it together. David tapped Hailey on the shoulder from his seat behind her in the log ride. "I hope your seat isn't as wet as mine," he joked, shifting his weight. "If it were any wetter, I'd be swimming."

Hailey had to laugh. She turned around and grinned. "My seat is nice and dry," she teased. She was surprised how easy it was to talk to David. She had been wondering what they would talk about on the ride, or even if they would talk at all.

"Well, I guess I'll be good and soaked by the time this ride is over," groaned David. They were beginning the climb to the final drop. Hailey's heart started beating faster. She didn't usually like rides like this one, but she hadn't wanted to appear too wimpy in front of Dylan. She didn't want him to be scared of a ride just because she was.

"Here we go, Hailey!" yelled David when they reached the top. The drop was quick and the great splash of water at the end was refreshing. When Hailey got out of the log ride, her legs felt like well-cooked spaghetti. She could have gone on that ride ten more times it was so fun!

By evening, Dylan was exhausted, so David carried him on his shoulders to the ferry. The line for the ferry was very wide, very long, and very crowded with hot and tired mothers, fathers, and children. Hailey stuck close to Alexandra, occasionally holding on to the handle of her straw bag when Alexandra looked the other way.

As they waited, Hailey shuffled her feet and squirmed uncomfortably: she needed to use the washroom, but she could see the ferry coming across the lake. If she went now, they would miss the ride back and have to wait even longer.

As soon as they were on the ferry, she turned to David and Alexandra. "I have to use the washroom," she said. "I'll meet you on the top level of the ferry." She hurried to find the restroom, not waiting for an answer from the Marcottes.

Hailey wrinkled her nose in the small washroom. Didn't they ever clean or use air fresheners? She used the toilet quickly, plugging her nose the whole time. When she exited, she saw there were a lot more people on the lower level than there had been five minutes before. She began making her way to the steps to the upper level, but there seemed to be obstacles everywhere—bikes, young teens on rollerblades, strollers, and buggies. Where were the steps?

It was so stuffy and smelly on the lower level, Hailey decided to stop and take a puff of her inhaler. But even after two puffs, her heart was still beating quickly and her breathing felt ragged. Hailey took a deep, shaky breath and looked around carefully. There! She spotted the stairs.

Getting up the stairs proved to be a chore, as well. Teenagers were sitting on the steps, blocking them. Why hadn't she just used the washroom on the island? She could have avoided the whole mess. Missing the ferry wouldn't have been so bad.

Once Hailey reached the top, her heart almost stopped: the top deck was wall-to-wall people. The bottom level looked roomy compared to the hundreds of people there. Where would the Marcottes and Dylan be?

Hailey clutched her small bag to her as she was jostled first one way and then another. Her heart was racing so fast it was all she could hear. The voices and shouts of people around her seemed muffled. Every time she took a step in what she thought was the right direction, she was pushed the opposite way.

Hailey shut her eyes and tried to remember what David and Alexandra were wearing. Had Alexandra taken off her big straw hat? Was David wearing a blue shirt with white pants? Was Dylan still on David's shoulders? With David being so tall, it would make them stand out for sure, Hailey told herself.

Suddenly, it got quiet. Hailey realized the operator of the ferry had shut off the engine, which meant they would soon be coasting slowly into the dock. She still hadn't found the Marcottes. What was she going to do?

Chapter Six

ailey fought back the panic rising in her. She reminded herself it was just a ferry. It wasn't as big as a mall with a whole bunch of ways out and multiple levels. There was only one way off the ferry—the lower level. Hailey shook her head. *No*, she thought, *I very clearly told them to meet me on the upper level.* But where on the top level were they?

Hailey pushed through the crowd and headed toward some benches. She climbed on one and stood up on her tiptoes. She would just wait there until she saw them. But even on her tiptoes, all Hailey could see were people's shoulders. She hoped desperately for a glimpse of David, Alexandra, and Dylan. She had just turned around when she felt a hand on her shoulder. She heaved a sigh of relief when she realized it was David.

"Thank God we found you," said David as he gave her a huge hug. "You did the right thing by coming to wait here. Standing on the bench made you a lot taller and easier to spot."

Seconds later, Alexandra and Dylan were also at her side. "I not like your hide and seek game," said Dylan solemnly.

"I didn't like it either," Hailey quietly responded.

Alexandra looked around. "We'd better get off now," she urged. "We're some of the last people still on the ferry."

On the way to the car, Hailey kept her eyes down and put one foot in front of the other, step by step. She barely heard Alexandra making a "what to do if we get separated on a trip" plan.

Hailey had never been so glad to sit safely in the back seat of a car. Dylan fell right asleep and the quiet ride home gave her time to relive her day. She had been expecting to have a miserable day, but aside from the maze and the ferry, it had been all right. The mini golfing had been fun and the weather had been perfect. Hailey had really enjoyed the rides and it was great she didn't have to spend the entire time watching and worrying about Dylan. It felt good to be herself and have a little fun.

When they returned to the Marcottes', Hailey couldn't stop yawning as she gave Dylan his medicine and put him to bed.

"Good night, Hailey. I love you," Dylan said. He wrapped his arms around her in a big hug.

"I love you too, Dyl," she whispered back.

Dylan sat up suddenly and looked over at the doorway. Hailey followed his gaze.

David and Alexandra were at the door. "Good night, Dylan," they said. "We had a great day with you and your sister. Sleep tight. See you tomorrow morning." The Marcottes quietly shut the door.

Hailey gave her brother one last hug before she went to her room. She fell asleep as soon as she lay down on the bed.

Hailey spent most of the next morning reading her snowboarding book and listening to her CD player on the Marcottes' back porch. From where she sat, she could easily see Dylan as he built massive sand castles in the sandbox. Alexandra was sitting on the edge of the sandbox helping him fill buckets with sand.

Hailey had just finished reading an article about waxing snowboards the organic way when Dylan ran up to her. "We get to go to the park that has swings and a climber and a slide and a little forest beside it!" he squeaked happily. "You get to come too! 'Andra said so."

Hailey looked up and readjusted her sunglasses. "That's really nice Dyl, but I'm very busy. I'll go with you another time."

She turned her attention back to her book. She was quite comfortable sitting and reading. She didn't want to go anywhere.

Alexandra walked over to her, brushing sand off her jeans. "Dylan really wants you to come along, Hailey. This isn't a choice for you. When we get back, we will have a hot dog lunch before Anna picks you up to go back to the Dunlops'."

Hailey stood up quickly, knocking her book down. "Fine, whatever. I guess we're living in a dictatorship."

Alexandra laughed. "Yup, sometimes living in a family means living in a dictatorship. A benevolent dictatorship, but a dictatorship nonetheless."

Hailey didn't dare respond to Alexandra's comment. She knew she would say things she'd definitely regret.

Dylan skipped all the way to the park, holding both David and Alexandra's hands and screaming with delight as they swung him in the air between them. Hailey fumed and dragged her feet as she followed behind. Living at the Dunlops' was no picnic, but at least Mrs. Dunlop wanted the kids to talk about their feelings. Hailey would bet if Dylan hadn't wanted to go to the park, Alexandra would have listened to him. It was so unfair! Maybe Alexandra didn't care about Hailey's feelings because she only cared about Dylan's. After all, Dylan was much cuter and friendlier than Hailey was, and, in Hailey's opinion, much more adoptable.

Hailey was so lost in thought she only looked up when she heard Dylan calling her to go down the slide. She hadn't realized they were already at the park.

"I'll go with you, buddy," said David, taking Dylan by the hand and heading toward the climber.

"Hailey, let's sit down on that bench. I owe you an apology," said Alexandra.

Hailey looked at Alexandra in surprise.

"I can tell by the way you've been dragging your feet, and the death glares you keep shooting me, I messed up," said Alexandra softly. "I'd like it very much if you told me what's going on in your head right now."

Hailey balanced herself on the very edge of the bench, lined up her feet perfectly with the edge of the grass, and thought about what to say. "You didn't give me a choice about the park. I was happy reading and you acted like you didn't care about what I wanted."

"I'm sorry I made you feel like I don't care about your feelings; I do, very much. It's just sometimes we need to spend time together so we can learn more about each other. You sitting alone reading doesn't help us get to know you. I shouldn't have made the smart remark about this family being a dictatorship. It isn't really, mostly it's a democracy, and we all get a say."

Alexandra stopped talking and patted Hailey's knee. "I hope my apology helps you feel better."

Hailey shuffled her feet in the dirt in front of the bench. "Yeah, I guess." Alexandra did make a good point about spending time together so they could learn about each other. She was glad Alexandra had picked up on her feelings and taken the time to talk to her and apologize.

Just then, David and Dylan came running over. "We just saw a coyote in the woods!" David exclaimed. "I heard there were coyotes in these woods again, but didn't actually believe it."

Dylan leaned into Hailey. "What's a coyote?" he whispered loudly.

"A coyote belongs to the group of animals that has dogs and wolves in it," explained David. "You can think of it as sort of a cross between a dog and a wolf. We have to be very careful to stay away from them.

They are actually more afraid of us than we are of them, but if they feel threatened, they will attack."

"I want to go home; I not like coyotes," announced Dylan.

"Good idea," said Alexandra. "I'm getting hungry for hot dogs."

Dylan grinned. "Me too. Can I have lots of ketchup on mine?"

"Of course you can," said David. "Let's head home. There won't be any coyotes in our yard to try and steal our hot dogs."

After lunch, Hailey was just putting her plate in the dishwasher when she heard Alexandra's cell phone ring.

Alexandra answered it. After speaking for a few minutes, she hung up. "That was Anna; she's going to be a little delayed getting here. It will probably be around 2:30, not right after lunch as we had planned."

Hailey shrugged. "That's okay," she said, "I know Dylan won't mind staying longer."

"What about you, Hailey, do you mind?" asked Alexandra quietly.

Hailey scuffed her sneaker back and forth. Right now, she wasn't sure how she felt. She had been looking forward to seeing Keisha again and discussing the weekend with her. A couple more hours here wouldn't be so bad, she supposed.

"Whatever," mumbled Hailey. She turned away from Alexandra.

Alexandra picked up the ketchup and put it in the fridge. "Why don't we play a game of Dominoes while we wait for Anna?"

Hailey carefully wiped down the counter before she answered Alexandra. "Dylan's too little to play a game like that. His favourite game is Candyland."

Alexandra went into the living room and returned with a brightly coloured Domino set with large cardboard pieces. "I think he just might be able to play this version with our help," she insisted. "If it turns out to be too frustrating for him, then we'll bring out Candyland."

Hailey choked back her anger. She wanted to ask them why they thought they knew everything about Dylan when they'd only spent two days with him, while she had spent her whole life with him! She knew she would only end up being rude, though, and she had no intention of looking at Alexandra's flashing angry eyes again.

"I don't feel like playing a game that I think is too hard for my brother," Hailey said. Each word came out between her gritted teeth.

"We know you love your brother very much and you're very protective of him, but we think he needs to have new challenges once in a while so he can expand his learning," responded David.

Hailey turned around and left the room. She didn't want to watch Dylan playing a game she hadn't taught him. She felt like she should have been the one to introduce a new, more challenging game. She had been taking responsibility for him for three years now, without anyone's help.

Hailey could hear Dylan admiring the beautiful colours on the cards as he counted the large dots on them. He was actually doing pretty well. She wished he would get frustrated with the game and prove her right. She picked up the disc player she had left lying on the couch, put the earphones in, and turned the volume up to drown out the sounds of the Marcottes playing with Dylan.

Hailey didn't look up until Anna arrived to pick them up. She managed to choke out, "Goodbye and thank you for having us," as they were leaving. Dylan needed to learn manners, after all.

"Are you going to be our new mommy and daddy forever and for real?" asked Dylan as he hugged David, and then Alexandra.

Hailey froze. She knew she had been a brat this weekend. They probably were going to change their minds because of her.

"Yes, we're going to be your real mommy and daddy," assured Alexandra with a huge smile.

Hailey let out a long held-in breath. At least she hadn't ruined Dylan's chances of being adopted. She was sure they were still going to discuss whether they really wanted her too.

That evening, back at the Dunlops', Hailey sat at her usual dinner spot and squirted some ketchup onto her macaroni and cheese.

"You haven't told me one single thing that happened this weekend," accused Keisha. She pretended to jab at Hailey's arm with her fork.

Hailey finished chewing. "Yeah, I know," she replied. "I thought maybe we could talk later." She looked around the table at the Dunlops and the other children.

Keisha grinned. "I know what you mean," she said. "I think we should be nice and do the dishes tonight, Hailey. Or does someone else want to scrub pots instead of us?"

Hailey smiled as everyone scattered from around the table, including Mr. and Mrs. Dunlop. "What a way to get some privacy," she moaned. "I can't stand doing dishes. Mrs. Dunlop always burns something," she complained.

"I know, I know," agreed Keisha. "But this way no one will dare come in the kitchen." She closed the kitchen door and lowered her voice to a whisper. "I have something really juicy to show you, but it has to be a total secret."

Now Hailey was curious. "What do you have that's so great?"

Keisha filled the sink with hot water and added a squirt of detergent.

"First you have to tell me about your weekend," she demanded. "Oh, and I want to borrow your disc player and the Katy Perry CD."

Hailey hesitated for a moment. "Don't you dare break my disc player or lose the disc," she warned. "I don't have too many good discs, you know."

"I know, you're such a poor little orphan girl," scoffed Keisha. She threw a dishtowel at Hailey. "Come on, start drying."

Hailey picked the towel up off the floor. "I might not be a poor orphan girl for long," she said. "I think the Marcottes really want to adopt Dylan and me. Well, Dylan anyway."

Keisha snorted. "Why not you? Did you tick them off or something?"

"They bought me some new clothes and I told Alexandra off about it," answered Hailey. "I also got really mad when they made me go to the park."

"You turned your nose up at new clothes?" asked Keisha, staring at Hailey in disbelief.

Hailey snorted and put her hands on her hips. It was just like Keisha to focus in on the clothes issue and ignore the rest of what Hailey had confided. "Well, would you want someone picking out all your new clothes?" she defended herself. "What if you didn't like them?"

"You could always exchange them," answered Keisha. "I'm sure they kept all the receipts."

"Anyway, we went to Centre Island," continued Hailey, ignoring Keisha's comment. She wasn't about to let Keisha know she had just made a good point.

"Canada's Wonderland would have been way cooler," Keisha said, wiping off the kitchen table. "Did you have any fun at all?"

Hailey put another dish on her growing stack. "Yeah, actually," she conceded. "Dylan sure did." Hailey twisted the dishtowel around her hand. "The only time he didn't have fun was when he, David, and Alexandra got lost on the ferry on the way back." Just remembering the ferry ride back was making Hailey's heart do jumping jacks.

"Since when do grownups get lost?" asked Keisha with a smirk.

"They got confused about where they were meeting me," mumbled Hailey. Keisha didn't have to know all the gory details. "We found each other just before the ferry docked, but it made me think: what's the point of getting all attached to new parents? I mean, look how fast we got separated. How do I know they're not going to get in an accident like my parents did and then Dylan and I'd be in the same boat as now?"

"Hey, back up the paranoid truck!" said Keisha. She turned off the tap. "What happened to your parents was a freak accident. Just because you care about other people doesn't mean they're also going to die." Keisha grabbed the towel out of Hailey's hands and snapped her legs with it.

"Ouch, you brat!" grumbled Hailey. She fell silent as they finished the dishes and she tackled the burnt pot. Overall, it had been a nice weekend. For a few moments, while she was sitting with Alexandra on the boulder outside the maze, she had pretended the Marcottes really were her parents. It felt nice to belong somewhere, to be a permanent part of a family.

"I have something you might like to see," reminded Keisha.

~ 63 ~

"Oh yeah, that juicy thing," remembered Hailey.

"First, the player and the tunes," demanded Keisha, her hand outstretched.

Hailey reluctantly handed over the disc player. "Here, I never took the Katy Perry disc out of it."

"Anna dropped a piece of paper out of her briefcase when she was dropping you guys off. I picked it up and, of course, took a quick look at it. Just to see if it was worthwhile, you know."

Hailey reached for the paper Keisha dangled. "Well, hand it over," she commanded. "This I have to see."

Keisha handed the paper to Hailey just as the telephone rang. Keisha answered, and immediately pulled up a stool to sit on. Hailey left the kitchen and peeked in on Dylan. She gave him his medicine and said good night to him, then headed to the room she shared with Keisha, flopped on her bed, and began reading.

Chapter Seven

The paper was dated with that day's date. Hailey squinted; she had to concentrate to make out Anna's handwriting. It looked like she had written on her lap or something. As Hailey read, she realized the whole page was filled with notes Anna had taken during a chat with David and Alexandra.

The first side of the paper contained notes about Dylan. The Marcottes enjoyed Dylan's cheerfulness and enthusiasm for life. They were also pleased Dylan was so comfortable with them. They didn't foresee any major discipline problems with Dylan. The page also included notes on what medication Dylan was taking and the concern he would become resistant to the antibiotics. He took them so often, his body would build up a resistance to them and they wouldn't be as effective. Anna had also written that Alexandra was glad her job at the hospital had given her plenty of experience in dealing with seizures in young children.

Hailey rolled over onto her back and took a breath before she tackled the other side of the paper. She would love to tell Anna to go back to school to learn to write properly. She turned on her bedside lamp and continued reading. Anna had written that the Marcottes were 'quite taken' with Hailey as well. They both admired her independent nature and were impressed with how well she took care of Dylan. But, there were also notes on her being aloof and unwilling to become involved in activities with the family. The Marcottes hoped that soon, Hailey would be able to become more involved and feel more a part of the family. David and Alexandra also hoped she would open up to them more and share what she was thinking, instead of covering up her feelings with rude behaviour.

Hailey was amazed. None of the other foster homes she had been in had ever appreciated her independent nature; they had all considered her independence a nuisance. And, she had been told more than once to go and have fun and not hover so much over Dylan. This was certainly an unusual viewpoint!

Hailey lay on her bed and thought about what the note said for a long time. It had gotten very late.

Keisha had quietly crept into bed earlier and fallen asleep as soon as she lay down. Hailey had heard the Dunlops putting Dylan to bed. She was glad she had taken a few minutes to give him his medicine and say goodnight to him. Hailey was just about to fold up the paper and put it away when she noticed she had missed something written in pencil on the margin of the page. It was a note about the Marcottes having Hailey and Dylan come to live with them in early September instead of later in October as originally planned. The Marcottes wanted them to be able to start in their new schools after Labour Day and not have to change again later. There was also a note that said the actual adoption would happen in late fall.

Hailey sat up with a start as she thought about what she had read. It meant they were going to live with the Marcottes in a week! She looked over at the luminous red numbers on her clock: 11:42 pm. It was way too late to go and wake up the Dunlops to find out when exactly in late fall the Marcottes were going to adopt them. How was she going to find out about the adoption without letting on that she had read some of Anna's notes?

Hailey fell asleep after she decided the direct way would probably work best to get information from the Dunlops.

The next morning, Hailey woke up as soon as she smelled the strong coffee Mrs. Dunlop liked to brew. She jumped out of bed, pulled on some old jean shorts, and a white T-shirt, quickly ran a comb through her hair, and headed into the kitchen.

"Good morning, Mrs. Dunlop," bubbled Hailey. "I was just wondering if Anna told you anything about our weekend visit with David and Alexandra?" She held her breath. She knew Mrs. Dunlop was much freer with information than Mr. Dunlop was, especially when Hailey was polite about her request.

Mrs. Dunlop wiped her hands on a kitchen towel. "Actually, dear, Anna is coming over today to discuss that with all of us," she stated. "You might have a new home as early as next week. Isn't that exciting?"

Hailey pulled out a kitchen chair and sat down. "We're just going to live with them, right? Do you know when they are actually going to adopt us?"

Mrs. Dunlop hung the towel on a hook by the sink. "Well, I don't know exactly when they will sign the adoption papers, but don't worry about that, dear. Everything will work out nicely. The Marcottes are lovely people."

Hailey didn't like the way Mrs. Dunlop dismissed her question and didn't answer it. She wanted an exact date for the adoption, not some vague nonsense about late fall. She had tried so hard to be polite, but it had been useless: Mrs. Dunlop didn't have any useful information at all! Hailey knew she wasn't being fair to her foster mom, but she couldn't stop her temper from taking over, and she let it fly. "I am not your dear, and don't tell me not to worry! Stuff doesn't always work out well. Did you forget why we're here? My parents died because of a drunk driver! Is that what you would call working out well?"

"Oh my, Hailey, there is no reason to get snippy," scolded Mrs. Dunlop.

"Anna is coming over after breakfast and will answer all your questions then." Mrs. Dunlop opened the cupboard and took down cereal bowls. "Now make yourself useful and set the table, please."

Hailey slowly placed the bowls on the table as she thought about what the meeting with Anna would be like. She was just pouring some flakes into her bowl when Dylan and Taylor came racing into the kitchen. Dylan was laughing loudly.

"You can't catch me, I the ginger boy man," he teased her.

Taylor dove around the table after him. "Oh yes, I can, gingerbread man!"

Hailey had to grab the cow-shaped pitcher of milk to keep it from tipping over as the two of them ran around and crawled under the large, kitchen table.

Meanwhile, Trevor, Dustin, and Keisha had made their way to the breakfast table as well. It was always so loud when Taylor and Dylan were playing. Hailey knew Mr. Dunlop's patience for their game would run out at any moment.

"That's enough!" Mr. Dunlop roared as if he sensed Hailey's thoughts. "I would like some peace and quiet while I read the paper." He sat down heavily in his chair and picked up the Retirement Living section of the newspaper.

Taylor and Dylan sat down, and Hailey couldn't help but snort as she looked over at them. Mrs. Dunlop had made the mistake of putting straws on the table. Taylor began by blowing milk at Dylan through her straw. Dylan eagerly picked up his spoon and flung a shredded wheat at Taylor. Hailey sighed as she thought back to the day Dustin had taught Dylan the fine art of flinging food off forks, knives, and spoons. That behaviour wasn't going to be nearly as fun at the Marcottes. Although the children in the Dunlops' home could aggravate each other to tears, they also had a great deal of fun together. They related well to each other knowing what it was like to be a foster child.

The kids had finished breakfast and Mrs. Dunlop had just finished helping Taylor and Dylan clean up their mess when Anna knocked at the door.

"Hi guys," Anna greeted them as she walked into the living room. She set her briefcase on the coffee table and opened it.

"Would you watch the children in the backyard, please Keisha, while we meet with Anna?" asked Mr. Dunlop.

"Sure; I don't have anything better to do," huffed Keisha before she hollered for Dustin, Trevor, and Taylor to go out to the yard.

"The Marcottes are looking forward to having you come live with them next week," began Anna, confirming Hailey and Dylan were going to live with David and Alexandra on Labour Day so they could start their new schools right away.

"So when are they actually going to adopt us?" asked Hailey.

"The court date hasn't been set yet, but once we get the judge's fall schedule, David and Alexandra will let you know. I'm going to guess late fall, early winter," explained Anna.

"It will be such an exciting day," added Mrs. Dunlop. "We will be coming along when you see the judge and the papers get signed."

Dylan had been playing with a paper airplane during the meeting. He jumped off the couch and went in pursuit of the plane he had thrown. "Are 'Andra and David going to be our new mommy and daddy?" he asked.

"Yes," said Anna and the Dunlops together.

Dylan picked up his plane and flew it around the room. "Now I get to sleep on my airplane sheets all the time with my new mommy and daddy!" he sang loudly, then ran out to the backyard.

Hailey glared over at Anna. "They could still change their minds. I don't think it's fair for you to tell him stuff like that when it might not happen. You should have told him that only maybe they'll adopt us."

Anna looked over at Hailey and frowned. "Hailey, I hope you won't share your negative ideas with Dylan; you're going to confuse him. He's happy about this move and you should be too."

Anna didn't wait for Hailey to answer her. "Honestly, I don't know what's gotten into you. You should consider yourself lucky," she continued as she stood up from the couch abruptly.

Hailey had never seen Anna so angry.

"You're behaving in a very selfish manner," Anna exclaimed. She snapped her briefcase shut, and stalked to the door. She said a curt goodbye to the Dunlops and left.

Hailey threw herself back against the couch. *I certainly have a knack for ticking people off*, she thought as she straightened the edges of the afghan draped over the couch. Hailey didn't want to get all excited about being adopted and then have it fall through. She didn't want to ever again feel that overwhelming disappointment she felt when the couple from a year ago, who were going to adopt her and Dylan, backed out. Hailey would rather not get her hopes up and then have them dashed.

The last week of summer passed very quickly. All too soon, it was Monday, the Labour Day before school was to start. The Marcottes would be picking Hailey and Dylan up after breakfast. Hailey grabbed her old blue duffel bag and tossed her clothes, inhalers, CDs, and disc player into it. She was about to put the journal in it when she remembered the piece of paper from Anna's briefcase. She picked it up from where she had stashed it between the pages of her snowboard book and reread it. Maybe everything was going to be okay; David and Alexandra liked her well enough. She would just have to be sure not to be too much of a bother so Alexandra and David wouldn't have to deal with her asthma. She also needed to remember to keep her temper in check.

Dylan flew into Hailey's room just as she was zipping up the duffel bag. "Look at me, I Superman!" he shouted as he flew around the room, a sheet draped around his shoulders.

Hailey put her duffel bag on the floor and gave her Superman a hug. "David and Alexandra will be here soon," she said. "Let's go check if you packed everything."

"Okay," Dylan agreed as he ran into the small room he had shared with Dustin. Keisha and Trevor had found a suitcase that was still in reasonable shape at a neighbourhood garage sale on the previous Saturday. The suitcase was packed with papers, his stuffed toys, and his treasured airplane books.

"Where are your clothes, toothbrush, and washcloth?" Hailey asked as she rummaged through his suitcase.

Dylan shrugged. "You can put them in your bag."

Hailey sighed, walked over to his chest of drawers, and opened them for the last time. She pulled out an armload of clothes and carried them over to her duffel bag. She was just stuffing them all in when she heard a light knock at the door.

Alexandra stood at the door. "Are you ready?" she asked.

"As ready as I'll ever be," answered Hailey with a smile. She bent to pick up a stray sock and wondered if the Marcottes were ready for her.

When it came to saying goodbye to Keisha, Hailey had to swallow several times to prevent tears from flowing. There was no way she was going to cry in front of Keisha.

"We can call each other you know," said Keisha. She handed a note with the Dunlops' number on it to Hailey. "Here, in case you forget," she joked. Hailey noticed as Keisha stuck both hands in the back pocket of her jeans and rocked back and forth on her heels. Hailey knew Keisha well enough to know she only did that when she was feeling unhappy and was trying to hide it.

Hailey spent the entire ride to the Marcottes' focussing on her breathing. She really needed her inhaler, but it was in her bag in the trunk of the car.

When they got to the Marcottes' house, Hailey ran up to her room, dumped her bag out on the bed, and took a puff of her blue inhaler.

Dylan came into her room. "We're going to have a family meeting about bein' a family," he declared importantly.

Intrigued, Hailey followed Dylan into the spacious living room. She settled down on a small woven rug by the coffee table and looked curiously at David and Alexandra sitting on the couch.

David cleared his throat. "We called this meeting because we wanted to, as a family, discuss the rules, responsibilities, and obligations each one of us has as a member of this family," he began. "We want to avoid any confusion about limits and boundaries in the future."

Hailey wasn't sure she liked where this meeting was going. Rules? Responsibilities? Boundaries? The meeting didn't sound like it would be any fun all; it felt like it was already the first day of school and the new teacher was laying down the law.

David went on, "There are only a few rules that we all need to remember. I've typed them out and they will be posted on the fridge."

David put the list down on the coffee table. Hailey moved over to the couch and had a look at it. The first thing she noticed were the pictures beside each of the rules. Even though Dylan couldn't read, he would be able to use the pictures to remind him of the rules. What a thoughtful idea! The pictures described each rule very well. There were five rules:

Always tell the truth.

Don't hurt yourself or others.
Have respect for each other.
Don't touch it if it isn't yours.
Talk it out if it bothers you so much
that you can't sleep at night.

David showed Hailey the other page he had printed out. It was a list of jobs around the house, for which Hailey and Dylan could earn a weekly allowance. Hailey hated housework. Her parents had always found a way to make helping out fun, but when they died, the fun of housework had died with them. It felt as if every time she was with the Marcottes, she was reminded of her parents. Hailey stood up, fists clenched at her sides. She knew she was overreacting, but she couldn't stop herself from thinking that the Marcottes just wanted two older kids around their house for slave labour!

If she looked at Alexandra and David, she knew she would lose her cool. The feel of her nails pressing into her palms kept her from grabbing that piece of paper and crumpling it up. "What if I don't do any of these jobs, ever?" she spat out. "I really don't care if you give me an allowance or not."

"It would be nice if you helped us out from time to time, but if you're unwilling, then we can't make you," stated Alexandra slowly. "You'll just have to live without allowance."

Hailey was stunned at how calmly Alexandra was reacting and her calm reaction was making Hailey's blood boil. She could feel her pulse throbbing in the side of her head.

"My mother never made me do chores and she never had to buy me to make me help her out," she said.

Alexandra stood up. "I'm not your mother and things are going to be different now than they used to be," she answered, her voice rising. "You'll be better off once you start to face that fact."

"That's right, you're not my mother, and you never will be!" yelled Hailey. "I hope you never adopt Dylan and me!"

She ran to her room, slamming the door behind her as hard as she could. How dare Alexandra talk like that to her! She obviously didn't know what it was like to lose a parent. Didn't she know how much the words "not your mother" hurt? Hailey curled up on her bed and sobbed. Suddenly, she sat up and dumped her duffel bag on the floor. She picked up her snowboarding book and grabbed Anna's paper from it. It sure didn't seem as if the Marcottes appreciated her independent nature now! Those notes were just a bunch of garbage. She tore the paper into as many tiny pieces as she could. She didn't stop until the bed was covered.

Hailey looked up as her door opened. Alexandra stood in the doorway, her mouth hanging open in astonishment. "What happened here?" she asked, hands on her hips. "What are you ripping up?"

For a moment, Hailey was at a loss for words. How was she going to explain this away?

"I was just so mad that I ripped up a piece of paper that was lying on the desk," Hailey admitted.

Alexandra sat down on the chair by the desk. "I made you furious and upset."

Hailey nodded.

Alexandra brushed at a speck on her blue capris. "I'm sorry; I had no right to say what I did. We're both in a new situation: you're adjusting to a new family and I'm adjusting to being a parent to you and your brother."

Hailey looked out the window and mumbled, "I'm sorry I yelled at you. It's just that sometimes I get mad so fast…" Her voice trailed off.

Alexandra smiled. "That's where you and I are similar. I have a temper myself and it's something I'm always working on. I find counting to ten before I react helps sometimes."

Hailey tucked a strand of hair behind her ear. "Sometimes I leave the room so I won't say anything I regret."

"I want you to know that I am trying to be a mother to you," Alexandra said, "but at the same time I know I can't replace your mom. There are times when I am going to do things differently than your mother did."

Hailey nodded and stood up. It made her feel better that Alexandra could relate to what it was like to have a temper. Suddenly, she realized how hungry she was.

"Thanks for the talk. Is lunch going to be ready soon?"

"Yes, we're having macaroni salad and fruit cocktail," answered Alexandra. They went into the kitchen where Dylan and David were, to start with the lunch preparations.

Chapter Eight

The next day Hailey almost missed breakfast entirely. She stood in front of her closet for nearly twenty minutes deciding what to wear. It was the first day of school. With any luck, she would be at this school a long time, and she wanted to make a good first impression on the teachers and other students. She hoped she would find someone to be her best friend.

Hailey was so deep in thought, she jumped when Alexandra poked her head in the room. "How about the black jeans with a white shirt?" she suggested. "It's simple and comfortable."

Hailey agreed the jeans were a good choice. She looked at Alexandra, already dressed for work in a pale blue hospital uniform. "I guess dressing for work is easy for you."

Alexandra grinned. "I only need to decide what colour to wear: blue, yellow, or white."

Hailey had to practically feed Dylan his breakfast. He was too worried to eat.

"What if I can't do the numbers and stuff?" He didn't wait for anyone to answer. "The teacher won't like me 'cause I don't know letters or anything."

Hailey interrupted him. "Of course the teacher will like you. You'll learn the numbers and letters at school because that's what school is for—to learn what you don't know."

"But what if..." Dylan persisted.

Hailey cut him off. "No buts."

David got up to clear the table. "You're going to do fine at school, Dylan," he reassured him. "Do you remember how well you counted when we played Dominoes?"

Alexandra abruptly jumped up from the table. "Has anyone seen my car keys?" she asked. "I don't want to be late for work. You guys are lucky you can walk to school."

Hailey thought for a moment. "Didn't you put them in your purse?"

"You're right," said Alexandra. "My purse is on the table by the door. What would I do without you,

Hailey?" Alexandra blew kisses to everyone and swept out of the house.

Hailey smiled. She was glad to see even though she had lost her cool with Alexandra yesterday, today Alexandra wasn't still angry with her. She had appreciated Hailey's knowing where the keys were. Hailey was going to make it a point to keep an eye on where Alexandra left her keys from now on.

David turned out the kitchen light. "Go brush your teeth now, please. We need to get going," he said. After brushing her teeth and helping Dylan with his, Hailey ducked into her room to pick up her backpack. At the last minute, she decided to put her sunglasses on; they looked cool and helped to hide how nervous she felt about starting middle school.

Dylan was just putting on his backpack as Hailey walked to the front door to put on her shoes. "It's not sunny in here," he said when he saw Hailey with the sunglasses on.

"I know," she answered, "this is my new look for a new school."

David looked at her and tapped his chin thoughtfully. "Have you heard the expression: the eyes are the window to the soul?"

Hailey knew the expression well. It had been one of her dad's favourite things to say. A wave of sadness so intense it made her shake swept over her.

"The glasses are helping me keep my windows shut and the drapes closed," she managed. Anger roared in to replace the wave of sadness; it was no business of David's whether or not she wore sunglasses to school!

"Suit yourself, Hailey," said David as he ushered her and Dylan out the front door and locked it behind him.

"Will you carry me on your shoulders all the way to school?" asked Dylan.

"Nope, little man. You're getting too big for that," laughed David.

Hailey felt her anger slipping away as she walked behind David and Dylan. Being angry around Dylan was hard.

"This week I'm going to walk both of you to school," explained David.

"When you're comfortable with it, you can walk to school on your own. I'll be here during the day working on my novel."

It was comforting to know David would be reachable at home. Hailey wondered what kind of book he was writing.

The ten-minute walk to Dylan's school gave Hailey a chance to think about what her first day of school would be like. Would she make friends? Would she fit in?

After Dylan was registered at his elementary school and had met his teacher, Hailey gave him a big hug goodbye. "I'll see you later, Dyl," she said. "Have fun."

Hailey's middle school was just across the road from Dylan's. The two-minute walk didn't give her any time to mentally prepare herself. Changing schools was something she had always detested.

She adjusted and readjusted her sunglasses outside the office where David was registering her.

Once she was registered and David had said goodbye, she stood out in the courtyard, watching the activity around her. Everyone was exchanging summer stories, and talking about who was dating whom. Hailey shuffled closer to the doors and tried to look as if she belonged. She shifted her backpack from her right shoulder to her left and back again.

When the bell rang, she hurried in, trying not to get crushed in the stampede of students heading through the door. All the sixth graders were to head to the gym, where they would be divided into their homerooms. It was so hot, loud, and crowded in the gym, Hailey almost missed her name being called.

After class schedules and locks for lockers had been handed out, Hailey found her locker and began to fumble with the lock, trying to get it to work. She had never used a combination lock before.

"Need some help?"

Hailey looked up to see two girls standing by her locker. "You're going to be late for the assembly if you don't get that lock figured out. Oh, by the way, cool shades. You got them at the new retro store, right?" enthused the taller girl.

"Uh, yeah," stammered Hailey.

"I'm Samantha," continued the tall girl, shouldering Hailey aside and reaching for her lock. She gestured toward her friend who was pulling her jet-black hair into a ponytail. "That's my best friend, Julie."

Samantha turned to Hailey. "It's right, left, right. You'll get the hang of it soon enough." Hailey opened her locker, stuffed her backpack inside, and closed it again, locking it.

Julie grinned at Hailey and shoved Samantha aside. "Sorry about her. She has no boundaries whatsoever." She clapped her hands twice. "Chop, chop, the assembly's starting any second."

The three girls walked to the auditorium together. Samantha kept up a steady stream of chatter the whole way. "This assembly is so boring. It'll be the principal yammering on and on, welcoming us all back and reminding us to respect each other's differences, to do our best with the academics, yadda, yadda, yadda."

The assembly was as boring as advertised. Hailey only heard bits and pieces of it; it was hard to concentrate with all the side conversations happening around her. It didn't help that Samantha kept up a running monologue throughout the assembly.

At one point, Samantha pointed out a stocky, short-haired teacher near the front. "That's Simms. She teaches Gym," she said. "My brother is starting grade eight and he says we better pray we don't get her. Apparently, she's a complete nightmare."

The morning went quickly. Hailey was glad to see Samantha and Julie were also in her History and English classes.

Later, at lunch, Hailey was picking at the egg salad sandwich Alexandra had packed for her when she felt a tap on her shoulder.

"My mom gave me two chocolate bars today; do you want one?" asked Samantha, plopping down beside her at the table. "I am *so* not looking forward to Gym class," she groaned. "Did you get Simms too?"

"Yeah, I did," answered Hailey.

The bell signalling the change of classes sounded, and as Hailey followed Samantha out of the cafeteria, she dumped her half-eaten sandwich in the trash.

After Geography came the dreaded gym class. It was their last class of the day. Samantha had been in all of Hailey's afternoon classes.

Hailey sat on the gym floor listening to the teacher describe the year's activities, and the uniform they were to wear to every class. Hailey hoped the rumours weren't true about Simms being a nightmare.

Samantha leaned over to Hailey and whispered, "Couldn't they come up with something more original than blue shorts and white shirts?"

Hailey smirked and responded, "Right? But what is she going to do if we forget our uniforms?"

At that moment, Mrs. Simms looked over. "You, in the white shirt and black jeans."

Hailey felt her face go red. Mrs. Simms was looking right at her and so was the rest of the class.

"Do you have something you'd like to share with the rest of us?" Mrs. Simms' voice was full of sarcasm.

Hailey was glad she still had her shades on. That way, no one could see the tears in her eyes. She blinked them away quickly. A funny Facebook post came to mind; it fit the situation well: "Obviously I'm whispering because I'd rather not share anything with the class."

Everyone laughed. Hailey immediately felt better.

Mrs. Simms didn't let up. "Oh, I see, Miss Sunglasses, you think it's funny to be mouthy. Anything for a laugh, right? That won't be tolerated in my class; don't let me catch you interrupting again. Oh, and you can take those sunglasses off, they will only get in the way during Gym."

Hailey took her sunglasses off. None of her other teachers had made a big deal about her wearing them. Of course, her story about the glasses being prescription and her having light sensitivity issues hadn't hurt her cause either. Hailey didn't think her cover story would work on Simms, however.

After Gym, Samantha and some other girls crowded around Hailey as they walked to their lockers.

A girl in striped leggings was sympathetic. "My sister said Simms is a witch, so don't feel bad. She treats everyone like dirt."

The girl's words were of little comfort to Hailey. Her asthma was acting up again; it always did when she was embarrassed or stressed, and the activities in Gym had involved a lot of running and jumping. She'd never survive Gym with her asthma getting in the way. And, after the way Simms had treated her, she didn't want to share anything about her asthma with that cow of a teacher. But how was she going to deal with the activities, her asthma, and Mrs. Simms?

Chapter Nine

Hailey was one of the first students out the door at the end of the day. She smiled to herself as she thought how great it was that all her teachers were giving their students a break and not assigning any homework on the first day.

When she got to Dylan's school, Hailey saw David was already there, leaning up against the wall of Dylan's classroom. He turned and smiled at her. "How was your day?"

"Not bad," replied Hailey. "We don't have any homework and I met a couple of really nice girls."

"Excellent," enthused David. "I'm happy your first day went well. Dylan's class will let out in five minutes."

Hailey could hardly wait to see Dylan. She hoped his first day had gone well. After five minutes, the bell rang and the door to the classroom opened; Hailey almost missed Dylan amongst all the children eagerly greeting their parents.

"Hey Dylan," she greeted him. "Did you have a good day?"

The smile on his face was huge. "My teacher's name is Miss Walker," Dylan replied. "She said she's glad she has a boy like me in her class," he continued.

"Why is she happy to have you in her class?" asked Hailey, taking hold of her brother's hand.

Dylan ignored the question as he pulled Hailey over to where his bag and jacket were hanging. "See, this is my hook," explained Dylan. "This is my name: D-Y-L-A-N," he chanted loudly.

Hailey was glad Dylan had a good day in his new school, but she found it hard to concentrate on what he was chattering about; she didn't even notice he hadn't answered her question. Her mind was too full of Mrs. Simms. She remembered the time she had a tough teacher like Simms, back in grade two. Her mother had reminded her that the strict teacher just wanted the students to do their best. Hailey hoped Mrs. Simms was being tough to help her learn, and not because she was mean.

At dinner that evening, Hailey made fork designs in her mashed potatoes as she pondered how she was going to get through another gym class.

"Hailey, you haven't told us anything about your first day," said Alexandra. "Did you enjoy the lunch I made you?"

Hailey looked over at Alexandra. She was pouring more gravy on Dylan's pork chop.

"My day was alright," answered Hailey. If she told Alexandra she had thrown half of the sandwich away, she'd probably get a lecture. What Alexandra didn't know wouldn't hurt her.

As she watched Dylan scooping peas one at a time onto his fork, Hailey had an idea: if she made her own lunch, she could put in the amount of food she wanted to eat. Hailey turned to Alexandra.

"Thanks for making the sandwich, but can I make my own lunch from now on? You're so busy in the morning, if I make my lunch that will help you out."

Alexandra put her milk glass down. "That would be helpful. I need you to promise me you will be sure to include a sandwich, fruit, cheese, a cereal bar, and drink in any lunch you make; you can't learn well on an empty stomach."

"Sure, no problem," lied Hailey. It sounded like a lot of food to cram in a lunch bag. If she timed it right, though, Alexandra would already have left for work and wouldn't see what actually went into Hailey's lunch bag.

"Oh, I'm going to need blue shorts and a white shirt for Gym," added Hailey.

Alexandra nodded. "When's your next Gym class?" she asked.

Hailey tried not to sigh. "Tomorrow."

"I think there might be a pair of blue shorts in one of your drawers," said Alexandra, "and you have plenty of white shirts," she continued. "Which reminds me: don't forget to take your red inhaler every morning, especially before Gym."

Hailey continued to press her fork into the top of her potatoes. "Yeah, yeah, I know," she mumbled. Her blue inhaler did the job just fine; if she had a few extra minutes in the morning, she'd take the red one, but Hailey seriously doubted she'd have extra time.

The next day Hailey met Samantha in the change room before Gym.

"Bad enough we have to start the day with Gym, I heard Simms makes everyone run laps as a warm-up before class even starts," groaned Samantha.

"Whatever," said Hailey, hoping Samantha wouldn't see how worried she was about the class.

At that moment, Mrs. Simms came into the change room. "Let's move—the bell's already rung," she commanded.

Hailey had to hurry to get to the gym; she didn't have time to dig her inhaler out of her bag and take a puff.

Samantha was right; they had to run laps. Hailey started at a fast walk. Her breathing already felt funny. If she could just avoid running, then she could keep her asthma under control. As she continued to make her way around the gym, she noticed Mrs. Simms had her head down, making notes. Maybe she could get away with just walking...

"You, walking around instead of running," shouted Mrs. Simms from across the gym. Hailey stopped walking. She had been sure the teacher hadn't been looking! Hailey's face felt hot. Was she the only one sweating?

"Since you think I'm a teacher of very little brains, you can run ten times around the gym while the rest of us take a break," said Mrs. Simms. "While you're at it, you can think about the fact I see and hear everything that goes on in my class, even if you think I don't."

Hailey clenched and unclenched her fists as she ran around the gym. Her face burned like it was on fire. By the time she was done, it felt like her lungs were on fire, as well.

"We're going to play dodge ball," announced Mrs. Simms. She tossed a ball up in the air. "We'll see how good your reflexes are. Everyone know the rules?"

Hailey took several deep breaths and looked around the gym. A few students nodded.

"Count yourselves off with either a one or a two," ordered Simms. "The ones are by the door and the twos go by the ropes." Hailey stayed in the back of her team and managed to avoid being tagged until the game was almost over. Her team lost.

After changing out of her uniform, she slipped into the washroom and took a puff of her blue inhaler.

Samantha was waiting for Hailey when she came out of the washroom. "Come on, Julie's in our math class. Her sister says Mr. Hetherington is the funniest teacher. That's good, 'cause I'm going to need all the humour I can get—I hate math."

"Me too," responded Hailey as they pounded up the stairs to their first math class.

Mr. Hetherington did like to crack jokes. "Good morning to all my new victims," he greeted the class.

Hailey flipped open the textbook he handed out. The questions didn't look as hard as she thought they would be. Maybe she would actually pass Math.

"We're having a quiz today," said Mr. Hetherington. "Don't even start with your mumbling and grumbling about how you didn't study or that you didn't know about it," he continued, "you weren't supposed to. Get used to it, because I like pop quizzes."

Hailey's pencil kept slipping out of her hand as she hunched over the ten-question quiz. She had to take off her sunglasses because she was sweating so much they were slipping down her nose; she hoped she would be able to answer at least some of the questions right. Luckily, it turned out the questions were mostly a review of last year's math. Hailey figured she would get a good mark on the quiz.

That evening, Hailey read the pages in the math textbook that Mr. Hetherington had assigned. As long as she followed the steps he had shown them, she could figure out the answers, but it was tough going— she needed a break. Hailey pushed her chair back from her desk and went to look out her window.

Dylan ran into her room. "'Andra's home," he declared. "She needs help unpacking the shopping." Dylan tugged on Hailey's arm. "Come on, she has ice cream!"

"I have homework, Dylan; you're a big boy—you can help her all by yourself."

David came to her rescue. "How about we both help unpack the groceries and let your sister finish her homework?"

Hailey sat back down and slumped over the desk. She decided to start on her English homework; she would rather learn a thousand vocabulary words than do five math questions any day.

When Hailey was finished her vocabulary, she looked over at the clock. Half an hour had gone by. It was quiet in the house. Too quiet. Dylan was constantly making noise, either chattering happily or playing loudly and enthusiastically with his toys. Hailey opened her door to go investigate. Suddenly, she could hear Dylan crying. She ran into the kitchen—groceries were still in bags on the floor and Dylan was sitting on Alexandra's lap; David was just wringing out a damp cloth and putting it on Dylan's forehead.

"What happened?" asked Hailey. "Did Dylan have a seizure?" She bit her lip and stuffed her hands in her pockets.

"Yes, Dylan just had a small seizure," answered Alexandra. "I think he's coming down with a cold. This is the beginning of flu season, and I suspect more than a few kids have runny noses in his class right now."

Hailey went over to Dylan and touched the back of his neck. He felt warm.

Dylan wiped his eyes and looked up at Hailey. "It's okay, Mommy 'Andra looked after me real good," he said, sniffling.

Hailey felt sick to her stomach. What was happening? How did she miss Dylan getting sick? If only she hadn't been so worried about her own problems!

She knelt by Dylan. "I'm sorry I wasn't paying enough attention to you Dyl," she apologized. "I've just been...busy."

Dylan didn't answer. He had shut his eyes and fallen asleep.

"Hailey, it's not your fault," said Alexandra softly. "You don't need to apologize. David and I have been paying close attention to Dylan. We've been giving him medicine for the fever. It's important for you to concentrate on your schoolwork."

Alexandra's words tumbled over Hailey like a waterfall. Everything sounded muffled.

Hailey got up and went to her room. She sat on her window seat and let tears trickle down her cheeks. Dylan had always depended on her to take care of him. She blew her nose. It had been a long time since she'd been anything but a mother to Dylan. The trickle of tears turned into Niagara Falls when she realized Dylan had called Alexandra "mommy." *How could he forget their own mother?*

Chapter Ten

Hailey abruptly wiped her tears away and went over to her desk. There was no point now in even finishing her homework.

"Hey, are you giving up on your homework?" asked David, who had come into her room.

"I'm just taking a break," answered Hailey, "I'll finish it after supper." Luckily, David didn't notice she had been crying; she wasn't ready to explain she was feeling upset because Dylan seemed to be replacing their mother with Alexandra. And wasn't that the whole point of getting adopted? To be part of a new family, with new parents? Dylan was ready to accept Alexandra as his mother, but for Hailey, accepting Alexandra as a mother meant replacing the perfectly good mother she once had. Hailey wasn't sure if she was ready to do that yet.

The next day after lunch, Hailey walked as slowly as possible toward the girls' change room.

Maybe Simms is sick and we'll have a supply teacher, she thought as she pulled on her white shirt.

No such luck. As soon as attendance was taken care of, Mrs. Simms blew her whistle. "Five laps everybody, now," she ordered.

Hailey began to walk quickly around the gym; she hoped she would blend in with everyone else who was running.

"Just what do you think you're doing?" asked Mrs. Simms as she tapped Hailey on the shoulder.

Hailey took a step back from Simms' angry red face and crossed her arms. "I'm power walking," she explained.

"I asked you to run, not power walk," said Mrs. Simms with a grim tone. "What makes you think you can make up your own rules?" she demanded.

Hailey remembered something her idol, a gold-winning snowboarder, had said. "I'm a free spirit," she quoted, "I make my own path."

"Free spirits are not appreciated in this class," said Mrs. Simms. "You can't make your own path until you've learned to listen and follow instructions. That goes for the rest of the class too." The gym teacher turned around and glared at the other students.

Hailey uncrossed her arms. "I'm ready to run now."

"I'm not finished with you," said Mrs. Simms. "This conversation isn't over until I say it's over."

Hailey remained silent. She was getting into a lot more trouble than she wanted. This was not the way things were supposed to go.

"I will be contacting your parents," Mrs. Simms assured, "you won't get away with disobeying the rules twice in my class. Start running. Now."

As Hailey began to jog around the gym, she made up her mind to speak with Simms after class; the last thing she needed was Simms calling David and Alexandra. That would ruin her chances of being adopted, she was sure. Who wanted to look after a kid in middle school who got in trouble the very first week?

So much class time had already been wasted, that Hailey had hardly run two laps before Mrs. Simms blew her whistle for the main activity. "Everybody listen up: today's active game is called Fruit Salad, it's a game where you need to think before you act. Everyone starts in the middle."

Hailey bent to adjust her sock as she thought about how she was going to approach Simms. She didn't want her teacher to think she was just making up any old excuse to keep her from calling David and Alexandra.

"Hailey, what does it mean when I say bananas?" asked Mrs. Simms.

Hailey jumped. What had Mrs. Simms said about bananas? She had been too busy worrying about talking to her after class to pay attention. Hailey figured that if she was in trouble, she might as well make the class laugh about it. She said the first thing that came to her mind. "Um, it means you're going crazy?"

The class laughed. Samantha grinned widely at Hailey from across the room.

"That's it. Go do ten push-ups and then sit on the bench," commanded Mrs. Simms. "I don't want to deal with you for the rest of this class."

Hailey slowly did her ten push-ups and then sat down. Simms thought she was a troublemaker and rude. Things were getting way out of hand. Hailey looked up at the clock. Her heart pounded when she saw there were only a few minutes left in class.

After class, Hailey lingered in the locker room, slowly changing out of her uniform. "You going to get dressed today or tomorrow?" joked Samantha, slinging her bag over her shoulder.

"You go ahead," answered Hailey as she finished tucking in her shirt. "I really need to talk to Simms and get on her good side."

"Yeah, that's probably a good idea," agreed Samantha.

Hailey headed back into the gym. Mrs. Simms was bent over her notes, going over them in pencil.

Hailey cleared her throat. "Excuse me," she began.

Mrs. Simms looked up. "You're going to be late for your next class if you don't get on with it," she said.

Hailey almost turned around and walked out right then, but she needed to try to repair the damage. Her parents had always told her to make at least three tries before giving up on something important.

Here goes try number one, she thought as she took her hands out of her pockets. "I'm sorry about the way I behaved today in class. You see, the thing is, I have asthma, and I didn't have a chance to take my inhaler before class because I didn't want to be late and when I don't...."

Hailey stopped mid-sentence when she saw Mrs. Simms hold up her hands in a time-out gesture. "Your English teacher would not appreciate that run-on sentence," said Mrs. Simms with a small smile. "Now just slow down and take it one thought at a time."

Hailey couldn't believe that Mrs. Simms had smiled. It was incredible how a smile made Mrs. Simms seem almost pleasant.

"Anyway, if I don't take my inhaler, I have trouble breathing when I run or do active things," continued Hailey. "That's why I wasn't running, and I was so busy thinking about what to say to you about it that I wasn't really paying attention when you were explaining that fruit salad game. Sometimes I just say stupid things without thinking," she finished.

"Let me guess, you don't want me to call your parents about today," said Mrs. Simms.

Hailey nodded.

Mrs. Simms stood up. "Let's have a look at this inhaler."

After Hailey had shown her the inhaler, Mrs. Simms looked intently at her. "I won't call home, this time, but don't step out of line again."

Hailey had meant to tell Mrs. Simms that David and Alexandra were her guardians, not her parents, but she was so relieved Simms wasn't going to call home, she decided to let it go.

"I won't be a bother in your class again," she promised.

Hailey couldn't stop herself from grinning as she headed toward her History class. Mrs. Simms had even given her a note, explaining why she was late. It felt like a huge weight had been taken off her shoulders. Hailey knew her parents would have been proud of how she had handled the situation by herself.

When Hailey arrived at Dylan's classroom door that afternoon, she gave David a big smile. "Guess what? I hardly have any homework."

David nodded. "What's got you in such a good mood?" he asked.

"I just had a good day at school," she answered. "Oh, I was wondering what kind of book you're writing?"

"It's a science fiction novel, about life on Mars," explained David. "I'm glad you're interested in my novel; an author is always more than happy to share with others what they're writing."

"Can I read it when you're done?" asked Hailey.

"Absolutely. I'd love your opinion on it. In fact, you can be my official proofreader."

When Dylan came out of his class, Hailey gave him a big hug. "You want to be a big boy and carry my bag?" she asked. "You can even put your pictures in it. There's lots of room."

Dylan crammed his pictures into Hailey's bag. "Miss Walker says I draw the bestest airplanes," he exclaimed. "And she says all good artwork has to go on the fridge—is there room on our fridge?" Dylan asked David.

David tousled Dylan's hair. "If there's no room on the fridge, we'll make room," he promised.

Dylan skipped all the way home, swinging Hailey's bag wildly around. He kept up a steady stream of chatter, telling David all about his day. Hailey frowned as she walked along, slightly behind them. She felt like Dylan was ignoring her. He hadn't even looked back once to see if she was still following. Hailey felt very left out. Dylan wasn't sharing his school stories with her at all! He just kept talking on and on to David.

That evening after supper, when Hailey went to her room, she realized she couldn't see her red inhaler anywhere. She had made up her mind to put the red inhaler somewhere where she would remember to take it, hoping if she took it all the time, she wouldn't always have to take her blue inhaler before Gym. She had left it right on her night table...or had she?

Hailey looked under her bed. No inhaler. She pulled her suitcase out from under the bed and opened it. Still no inhaler. Maybe it was in the pocket of her pants. *No, not there either.* Hailey slammed her closet door shut. In her frustration she slammed it shut twice more.

Alexandra came into the room. "What are you doing?" she asked.

"The door must have slipped out of my hand," lied Hailey.

Alexandra didn't look very convinced. "If you let the door slip out of your hand again, I won't be able to believe it's accidental," she warned her. "If something's bothering you, you need to talk about it, not slam doors." Alexandra sat down on the bed. "I'm all ears if there's something you'd like to share."

Hailey almost sat down and told Alexandra the truth. She really wanted to, but the adoption wasn't final yet. She knew they still had to go to court to speak with the judge and sign the papers. She didn't want Alexandra to know she misplaced her inhaler; she was certain her carelessness with her medication would ruin her chances of getting adopted.

Hailey put on her most sincere face. "Really, everything's okay," she said.

"All right then," said Alexandra, standing up.

After Alexandra left the room, Hailey sank down on the bed. *Now what*? She couldn't imagine what David and Alexandra would say about her not taking her inhaler, let alone losing it!

Hailey tossed and turned for hours that night. Maybe this was another situation she could handle on her own, without involving the Marcottes. Where could her red inhaler be?

Chapter Eleven

ailey tried to keep from yawning as she sat at the breakfast table the next morning.

"Your eyes look puffy," said Alexandra. "Did you not sleep well last night?" she asked as she shifted her keys from one hand to the other and took a close look at Hailey.

Before Hailey could answer, Dylan jumped out of his chair. "I forgot! Today is Show and Share," he announced. "I want to bring my airplane pop-up." Dylan left the table in such a hurry, he pulled a corner of the tablecloth down and his cereal bowl fell on the floor.

While Dylan and David cleaned up the mess, Hailey put on her shoes and stuffed her lunch in her backpack. "I'm ready to go," she announced. She was glad Alexandra hadn't yet noticed that she had just been stuffing an apple and cheese and crackers in her bag every day for lunch. It had been hard to eat lunch this week with all the mess with Mrs. Simms.

"Wow, it's nice to see you so eager to get to school," said David. "You need to eat more breakfast than that, though. You only ate two bites of your Cheerios." He handed Hailey a banana and a cereal bar. "You should have time to eat those on the way. We're not going to make a habit—"

Dylan's loud chanting interrupted David. "I have a secret, I have a secret! You don't know what I'm bringing to school!" Dylan was jumping around, waving his book.

David took Dylan's book out of his hand. "We'll put this in your bag after your coat is on," promised David.

"I know what your secret is—it's your special airplane book," said Alexandra. She hugged Dylan and headed out the door.

When Hailey got to school, she opened her locker and shuffled her books around, looking for her gym shorts and shirt.

Samantha tapped her on the shoulder as she walked by. "Whatcha looking for?" she asked.

Hailey rummaged some more. "I think I forgot my uniform," she groaned. "How badly is Simms going to kill me for this?"

"She's not going to kill you—she's only going to torture you until Christmas," said Samantha, laughing.

Hailey bit her lip as they walked together into homeroom. By the time class was about to start, she was a nervous wreck. She walked into the gym feeling as if she were walking on eggshells. With hands thrust deep into her pockets, she approached Mrs. Simms.

"I'm really sorry, but it was kind of crazy in my house this morning and I forgot my gym uniform," she explained.

"Consider yourself lucky," said Mrs. Simms, after looking at Hailey for a long time. "I'm in a good mood today so I'll let you off with a warning. Don't ever come into my class again without a uniform. If you forget again, I will call your parents."

Hailey took her hands out of her pockets. "Thanks, I won't forget again."

Hailey was so relieved she skipped to her next class.

That evening, Hailey was sitting on her windowsill, reading one of the short stories she'd been assigned for English class, when Alexandra came into her room, still wearing her hospital uniform. "Keisha's on the phone for you."

Hailey took the phone and stretched the cord as long as it would go. It stretched right into the hall closet, so she sat in the closet with the door shut for privacy.

"Hey, Keisha, how's it going? How'd you even get this number?" asked Hailey.

"The Dunlops gave it to me, you dill weed," answered Keisha. "I have some great news! They tracked down some aunt of mine; she wants me to go live with her!"

Hailey sat up and twisted the phone cord around her baby finger tightly. "That sounds great," she mumbled. "I hope it works out for you."

"So what's it like living with a new family?" asked Keisha. "I mean, is it going to be hard for me?"

"It'll be easy," answered Hailey. "You don't have any brothers or sisters making it hard for you. Dylan is getting all lovey-dovey with David and Alexandra. He hardly even talks to me anymore. All he cares about is what he's bringing for Show and Tell, and ignoring me."

"Oooh, Show and Tell? I remember that! Don't you mean Bring and Brag? You're being stupid again, by the way. Dylan would never ignore you," said Keisha. "He's just getting used to living in a new place. Remember how he first followed Mrs. Dunlop around?"

Hailey wiped her sweaty hand on her jeans. "Yeah, but at least he didn't go around calling her mommy," she answered.

There was a brief silence on the other end of the phone. "Oh, I guess that's okay," said Keisha. "After all, the Marcottes are your new parents now. Dylan's little. He needs to call somebody mommy."

"It's not that I care whether he calls Alexandra mommy, it's just that I feel like he's forgotten that we had a real mom," responded Hailey quickly.

"You like to make things complicated," Keisha groaned. "Be glad you're his sister and not his mother."

"Yeah, but..." Hailey didn't get to finish her sentence; the line went dead in her hand. Hailey crawled out of the closet and hung up the phone.

Alexandra was putting a clean pile of laundry on Hailey's bed. "You don't have to hide in the closet to talk to your friends," said Alexandra. "We'd be glad to buy you a cell phone."

"You'd actually buy me a phone?" asked Hailey, grinning hugely.

"Sure, but there would be some rules and restrictions regarding it," answered Alexandra.

The phone rang again. Hailey jumped to pick it up. "Hi Keisha, what did you hang up on me for?" she grumbled.

"Trevor accidentally unplugged the cord," explained Keisha. "I've got to go now anyway. Talk to you later. Don't obsess over every little thing."

Hailey went into the kitchen. Dylan was smiling. "Hailey, I helped Alexandra make supper," he said. "I put on the secret 'gredient: chips!"

"That's great, Dylan," said Hailey. "Did everyone like your show and tell?"

Dylan looked over at David and frowned. "I got in trouble," he pouted.

"Hailey, we need to have a chat about why Dylan got into trouble," said David. "We'll discuss it after supper, though."

Hailey sat down at the table. How was she supposed to enjoy dinner now? What did Dylan do? Why did it concern her? She ate most of her dinner, but it all tasted like soggy cardboard with salty chips on it.

Hailey reached over to wipe Dylan's mouth. "You have a piece of tuna on your lip," she said.

Dylan moved his face away. "I can do it," he said. "I'm big."

"Fine," said Hailey as she threw her napkin down. She was hurt that he was rejecting her help. He had always let her clean him up before.

After supper, Hailey went into Dylan's room. "It's time for your Friday night bath and hair wash," she said.

Dylan continued playing with his Lego Duplo. "Look, David showed me how to make an airplane," he said. "Now I'm making an airport."

"That's nice," answered Hailey. "I'll run the bath while you finish." She headed for the bathroom.

"No, I want Mommy 'Andra to give me my bath," insisted Dylan. "She can make my hair look funny with the shampoo."

"So can I, Dyl," said Hailey. It was just like she had said on the phone to Keisha; Dylan didn't want her anymore, he only wanted Alexandra.

Dylan sat up and held out a blue block. "Here, you make the sky."

"It's time for your bath and Alexandra's not around, so I'll start filling the tub," insisted Hailey, her voice rising. What was this? Ignore your sister night? Giving Dylan his bath had always been a task she loved doing, and now he wasn't letting her do that anymore!

Dylan stood up. "No, only Mommy 'Andra can give me baths now," he insisted. "But you can still play with me."

Hailey fought back tears. Dylan was making it very clear he didn't need her anymore. "Fine, you're a selfish little brat!" she yelled. Yelling helped to hold back her tears. Dylan started to cry.

Hailey slammed his door shut and ran to her room. What a selfish little brother! If he didn't need her, she was never going to speak to him again!

David walked into Hailey's room. He had Dylan by the hand. Dylan was wiping away tears.

"We're going to solve this right now," said David. "Dylan tells me you yelled at him and called him a brat. We don't call each other names in this house."

Hailey looked down. She had made her brother cry. She had never made him cry before. She felt horrible.

"I'm sorry, Dylan," she said. "I didn't mean to yell at you. I'm just so used to giving you your bath that it's hard for me to change. I'm glad Alexandra can make your hair look goofy; it's a special skill."

Dylan smiled. "You can still give me my medicine," he said. "Only you can fly airplanes so good."

Hailey hugged Dylan and then began her homework while Alexandra gave Dylan his bath and tucked him into bed.

Hailey was finishing her last math question when David and Alexandra came into her room. "We would like to talk to you about what happened with Dylan at school today."

"Oh, yeah," answered Hailey. "I forgot."

"Do you know where your red inhaler is?" asked David.

Hailey rolled her pencil back and forth over her notebook. "No," she admitted in a quiet voice.

"How long have you been missing your inhaler?" asked Alexandra.

"I'm not sure," responded Hailey.

"Dylan found your inhaler," said David. "He brought it to school today. He was so proud of his find that he showed it to me just before I dropped him off."

Hailey was stunned. She had no idea what to say.

"Dylan could have gotten very sick had he decided to take some puffs of your inhaler," said Alexandra. "We're lucky David caught him before he hurt himself. You need to tell us if you're missing your medication," she continued. "The cold weather is coming soon and you know cold air makes your asthma worse."

Hailey nodded. She couldn't speak. She had really messed up. She twisted her hair around her finger and concentrated on not throwing up.

"Obviously you're not taking care of your inhaler properly if you can just misplace it like that for days," scolded David. "There is no way we can take you on a snowboarding trip in cold winter weather if you can't handle the responsibility of taking and caring for your inhaler."

Hailey folded a scrap of paper on her desk into a tiny square.

"If something like this happens again, we won't be going snowboarding at all this Christmas," warned David.

"Is there anything you'd like to say to us?" asked Alexandra. "You've been awfully quiet."

Hailey wanted to ask David and Alexandra if they still wanted to adopt her, but how could she? What were they going to say? You don't tell a kid to her face you don't want her! The other couple, who had backed out on Hailey and Dylan before signing final adoption papers, had simply said that it wasn't a good time for them to adopt two children.

David and Alexandra left the room. Hailey had screwed things up badly. Not only had she made Dylan cry, now she was in huge trouble with Alexandra and David. They couldn't trust her to look after her own inhaler. She knew that saying the snowboarding trip would be cancelled really meant they wouldn't be adopting her. If she screwed up again, her life might as well be over!

Chapter Twelve

Hailey swept everything off her desk and put her head down. Her breathing was getting to her again, so she pulled her inhaler out of her backpack and took two puffs.

She had just decided to pick up the books when Alexandra opened her door again.

"What hurricane blew through this room?" she asked.

Hailey bent to pick up the books. "I threw them off. I was frustrated." Hailey was tired of lying. It didn't get her anywhere, it just seemed to make things worse.

Alexandra nodded and sat down on the broad window ledge. "It looks like your temper ran away with you again," she murmured. "Is there something else bothering you?" she asked. "Your feelings are very important to me."

Hailey shifted on her chair. She desperately wanted to know if the Marcottes were still going to adopt her. She picked up her pen and clicked it several times before she began speaking. "Dylan's ignoring me all the time," she said. "He won't let me help him at all with anything. It's like I'm not good enough for him anymore. I guess that kind of hurt me, so I got mad."

Alexandra nodded. "You've been like a mother to Dylan and now he doesn't see you in that role anymore. It must hurt not to feel needed in that way."

Hailey looked up. "Yeah, I guess," she agreed.

Alexandra stood up. "You still have an important role to play with Dylan. No one else can ever be his big sister but you."

Hailey looked up and smiled. Alexandra's words reassured Hailey. It was true. No one else could be Dylan's older sister but her.

Later, as she lay in bed, Hailey reached into her night table drawer. She switched on her light and looked at the photo of her, Dylan, and their mother and father at the park. It was the last photo taken of the four of them together. Hailey carefully held the picture by its tattered edges. She felt tears coming down her cheeks. She missed her parents so much! She asked herself for the millionth time why they'd had to die. Quickly, she put the picture away. She didn't want the photo getting more ruined than it already was. It was the only concrete thing she had left of her parents.

The next morning, Hailey woke up when Dylan leaped onto her bed. She sat up. "Hey, you don't need to bounce like that," she groaned. "I'm getting seasick."

Dylan didn't stop jumping. His face was so close Hailey could smell the toothpaste on his breath. "Wake up, wake up, wake up!" he chanted.

"Oh, alright," she grumbled.

Dylan jumped off the bed, his task for the day done, and ran out of the room. Hailey got out of bed with a groan. So much for sleeping in!

At breakfast, she tried to read one of the short stories her English teacher had assigned the class. Alexandra tapped Hailey's hand.

"Don't spill any food on the book; I'm glad you're reading, but remember that is the school's book."

Hailey shut the book. Dylan was making too much noise to concentrate anyway.

"Does anyone want to come shopping with me?" asked Alexandra as she flipped through a grocery flyer.

Dylan slurped the rest of the milk out of his cereal bowl and pulled the flyer from Alexandra's hand. "I want to come. Can you buy me these ones?" He pointed to a picture of a brightly coloured lunch package that had hot dogs in it.

"I'll think about it, but I'm not making any promises," answered Alexandra as she took the flyer out of Dylan's hand.

Hailey yawned and stretched as Alexandra and Dylan headed out the door.

David looked over at her and grinned. "Ah, now we get some peace and quiet," he said. "Do you want some help with your homework?"

"Thanks, but I'm really okay," she answered. "I'm going to start on it now."

"In that case, I'll be cleaning the kitchen and then I'm going to work on my book," said David as he cleared the table.

Hailey had made her way through all of her homework but math when she heard Dylan and Alexandra returning. She peered out into the living room.

Dylan sounded upset. "You don't like me," she heard him complain. "How come you're so mean you didn't buy me those hot dogs?"

Alexandra dropped her keys on the dining room table. "I love you and I don't want you filling up on junk food for lunch," said Alexandra firmly.

Dylan stamped his foot and crossed his arms over his chest. "You're still mean," he pouted.

Hailey smiled as Dylan stomped right past her and went into his room. So, Dylan wasn't impressed with his precious Mommy 'Andra!

"I have a great idea," said Alexandra, turning to Hailey. "Would you like to head to the mall and see if we can find you a cell phone?"

Hailey grinned. "That would be great!" She went to put on her jacket while Alexandra told David that it would be a girls' afternoon out and there was leftover soup to reheat for lunch.

At the mall, they passed an outdoor sports store advertising a sale on snowboards. Alexandra stopped in front of the store. "Let's have a look around in here after we buy the phone," she suggested.

After they had left the tech shop, Hailey carried the bag with her new cell phone in it. "Thanks for buying me the phone," she said.

"David and I are glad to do it," answered Alexandra. "Remember, though, part of your allowance will go to pay part of the monthly contract for it."

"I know, I know," responded Hailey.

They headed back to the sports store. Hailey thought she was in heaven—one wall of the store was devoted entirely to snowboards. A board near the back of the store caught her eye—it had a beautiful snow scene on it.

"Alexandra, over here!" called Hailey. Alexandra hurried to the back of the store. "It's thirty percent off," Hailey said as she reached out to touch the snowboard.

Alexandra bent in for a closer look. "That's because it's a discontinued model. It's a good deal; I think we'll put it on layaway."

"What's layaway?" asked Hailey.

"The store will keep the snowboard for us for a small monthly fee until we're ready to pay for it entirely," answered Alexandra. "I don't want to make such a large purchase for you until I see that you are taking good care of yourself and your inhaler."

Hailey's heart was beating fast with excitement. No one had ever bought her something so expensive before! She couldn't even remember her parents buying her such a large gift! As she hovered by the cash register waiting for Alexandra to complete the layaway arrangements, Hailey imagined herself whooshing down the slopes on the board. She had her asthma completely under control. That snowboard would be hers very soon, she was sure.

"Spending money always makes me hungry," joked Alexandra. "Let's try out the new sub place."

"Sure," agreed Hailey.

Hailey enjoyed sitting in the food court with Alexandra. It was easy to talk to her, and they never seemed to run out of things to say.

That evening, after supper, Hailey took her phone out of the box and set it up. Now all she needed was someone to share her good news with!

Hailey smiled to herself as she dialled Samantha's number. They had become good friends over the last week. Besides not asking her a lot of personal questions, Samantha could make her laugh until her sides ached.

"Yo, Samantha, what's up?" asked Hailey when Samantha came on the line.

"Not much," answered Samantha. "You sound really happy."

"Yup," said Hailey. "I got a new snowboard today and a new phone!"

"Your own phone!" shrieked Samantha, so loudly Hailey had to hold the phone away from her ear. "How cool! I totally need to work on my parents for my own phone."

Dylan came running into Hailey's room. He was waving a large white sheet of paper. "I've got to go," said Hailey. "My brother's waving a big piece of paper around in my room. I'll see you Monday."

"Later," answered Samantha.

Hailey hung up and grabbed Dylan's arm. "Hey, what's that you're waving around?" she asked.

"We're having a family meeting again," answered Dylan. "In the living room in two minutes."

Hailey frowned. The last family meeting had gone badly. What was this meeting about? More rules? Maybe they were cancelling the ski trip. Maybe the Marcottes were going to send her and Dylan back to the Dunlops after all. The meeting could be about anything. But she really didn't want to go into the living room. She didn't want to hear about rules or bad news.

Things were just starting to look up. Hailey's feet felt heavy as she slowly walked into the living room. What was going to happen now?

Chapter Thirteen

Hailey sat down on the couch and looked up expectantly at David and Alexandra.

"We think you'll like this family meeting," said David, with a huge smile.

Hailey leaned back and heaved a sigh of relief.

"We just wanted to let you know the court date has been set to sign the final adoption papers," announced Alexandra.

Hailey sat up and looked over at Dylan. Did he understand what was going on?

"Did you explain about court and signing papers to Dylan?" asked Hailey.

"Yes, we did," answered Alexandra. "We put it in terms Dylan could understand easily. Our court date is set for five weeks before our trip to British Columbia."

Hailey felt as if there was a swarm of butterflies flying around in her stomach. She chewed on the ends of her hair as she wondered what the judge was going to say when they went to court. What was he going to do? Would it be like on television, with a jury of people who decided whether or not Hailey and Dylan were adopted?

"What exactly is going to happen when we go to court?" asked Hailey. "Are we going to be on trial?"

"No," answered David. "There will only be the judge. We'll just talk to him, explaining why we want to be a family, and then Alexandra and I will sign the papers. Then we will officially be a family."

Dylan jumped up on Hailey's lap. "Look at the big picture I drew!"

"Tell me about your picture, Dyl-Pickle," Hailey joked.

"I am not a pickle," said Dylan, arms crossed over his chest. "I am a people."

Hailey laughed. "I know; I just like having fun with you, Dylan. Wow! It looks like you covered that whole, big page. You were working hard."

"Yeah, I drew you and me and Daddy David and Mommy 'Andra sliding down the hills on our snowboarding trip," he said, jumping off Hailey's lap to point out everyone in his picture.

"That's really nice," assured Hailey distractedly. There were still two and a half months until the court date; time was going to go so slowly. Hailey made up her mind not to hold her breath about the final paper signing. She would just do her best, wait, and see what happened—she was determined not to get her hopes up.

On Thursday morning of the following week, Hailey was in math class, doodling in her notebook. The morning announcements were on. She had just finished drawing a perfect spiral when she heard the words, "...field trip for all grade sixes." Hailey looked up. Mr. Hetherington was handing out a stack of papers. She read hers as soon as it was passed to her: the grade six classes were going to the Ontario Science Centre!

"Hey, what's this Science Centre thing all about?" whispered Hailey to Samantha.

"Oh, it's really cool," answered Samantha. "It's like a museum, but you can touch and play with everything."

Hailey thought about the trip all day. It sounded like fun. That evening at dinner, Hailey pulled the permission form for the Science Centre out of her pocket and handed it to David. "We're going on a trip the first week of November."

David looked over the form. "We'll sign this after supper," he said. "It sounds like fun. I always enjoyed going to the Science Centre."

Hailey grinned. "Thanks. I'll do the dishes when we're done," she volunteered. She wanted to make sure David and Alexandra were in good moods and didn't change their minds about signing the form.

As Hailey washed the dishes, she thought about how Gym had not been a problem the past week. She had remembered to take her red inhaler every day and made sure she had plenty of time to have a puff of her blue inhaler before class. If she could keep this behaviour up, there was no way Alexandra would decide not to get the snowboard!

The following Monday was a hectic morning in the Marcotte household. Hailey was frantically completing History questions she had forgotten about.

"Hailey, get a move on!" David shouted. "We need to leave in ten minutes."

"Alright, alright," Hailey yelled back. She jammed her books and papers into her backpack and ran into the kitchen. There was no time for breakfast.

Hailey was tying up her laces when Dylan suddenly grabbed her hand. "My tummy feels yucky," he said. Then, he was throwing up.

"I've got this, Hailey," said David as he led Dylan over to the kitchen sink to start cleaning him up. "You go to school. Dylan's staying home with me."

Hailey was worried. "He probably has a fever."

"Don't worry. I'm giving him medicine for the fever now and I know what to do if a seizure does come on," said David. "Don't forget, I've programmed our home number into your phone. You can call me at lunch to see how everything is going."

Hailey left for school, worrying the whole way. It was a good thing there were no pop quizzes because she didn't hear anything that went on in any of her classes that morning.

Hailey was counting the minutes until she could call home; lunch couldn't come fast enough. When it finally arrived, she hurried to the lunchroom on wobbly legs. Hailey felt very sweaty and her hands were shaking. She was just fumbling around in her pocket to pull out her cell phone when she started seeing spots in front of her eyes and began to feel very dizzy.

Suddenly, she felt herself falling back against the wall. "Hey, I've got you!" exclaimed Samantha. "You need to sit—you look like you're going to pass out!"

Hailey slid down the wall and landed with a bump. At once, a crowd of kids were hovering over her.

"Out of the way, guys; show's over." Mr. Hetherington came over and knelt down by Hailey. "It looks like we have a case of 'no breakfast-itis'—nothing some quick sugar and a decent lunch won't fix."

Samantha pulled a chocolate bar out of her bag and offered it to Hailey.

"Here, eat this. You'll feel better. Remember, like that professor in the *Harry Potter* movies always says, chocolate helps."

Hailey took the chocolate bar Samantha had already unwrapped for her and took a bite.

"I'm calling home, Hailey," said Mr. Hetherington. "You're going to have the afternoon off."

"No," grunted Hailey around a mouthful of chocolate. "Our home phone is broken." She could not have David and Alexandra find out about this! It was going to come out that she had skipped breakfast this morning. Hailey knew how important eating properly was to the Marcottes; she didn't want to think about what they would do if they found out!

"Last I checked parents also have cell phones. I'll be able to reach them on those," answered Mr. Hetherington. He headed out of the cafeteria.

Hailey closed her eyes and leaned back against the wall. She had made such a mess of things! She wished she could put her sunglasses on, but she had left them on her dresser at home. She hadn't felt the need to wear them for at least a week. Now, though, she wanted to wear them as a shield.

Fifteen minutes later, David arrived with Dylan in tow. Mr. Hetherington was with them. Hailey heard him explaining what had happened and that he felt it would be best for her to rest for the afternoon.

"Come on, Hailey, let's get you home and resting," said David.

"I hope you feel better," said Samantha.

"Did Dylan have a seizure? Is he okay?" asked Hailey as they walked home. All she could think about was Dylan.

"He's okay. He has the flu, but the medicine did its work and brought the fever down fast. We're more worried about you. As soon as we get home, you're eating lunch."

Hailey had just finished lunch when Alexandra arrived home. After giving her a hug and making sure Dylan had an afternoon nap, she and David came into Hailey's room.

"We need to talk about what happened." Alexandra sounded serious. "Your math teacher figures you passed out because you didn't eat any breakfast. Is that right?"

Hailey leaned back against her headboard, holding her pillow in her lap. "Yeah, but it was busy this morning. Dylan threw up. I didn't have time."

"You would have had time if you hadn't dawdled so long in your room," said David. "What was taking you so long to come to the breakfast table?"

Hailey hugged her pillow tightly to her and didn't answer. She was already in so much trouble; she didn't want to admit she had been doing homework that she should have finished the night before.

"What's the number one rule in this family?" asked Alexandra.

"Always tell the truth," answered Hailey.

"Then out with it, right now," demanded Alexandra.

Hailey mumbled down into her pillow. "I forgot to do some History questions and I was finishing them up."

"Thank you," said David. "Now let's talk about what you've been eating for lunch. You only had one apple and a package of cheese and crackers in your lunch bag today. Is that all you've been taking for lunch?"

Hailey nodded.

Alexandra leaned forward from the chair she was sitting on. "Why did you break the promise you made to me to bring a proper lunch every day?"

Hailey could feel a tear slipping down her cheek. "I didn't think I could eat everything you wanted. I've been so nervous starting a new school that it's been hard to eat."

Tearfully, Hailey went on to tell them about her problems in Gym and explain how she had solved them. It was a relief to finally get everything out in the open and not have secrets anymore.

David groaned. "Oh, I completely forgot to let the office know about your asthma! I'm sorry you didn't feel you could confide in us, Hailey. However, I am glad you worked it out on your own."

"Thanks," answered Hailey.

"I'm sorry you went through all of that alone. Can you promise me that you will share more of what's happening at school with me? I care deeply about you and want to help," said Alexandra.

"You're not mad at me?" asked Hailey. "I thought for sure you'd ground me or something."

"No, I think you feel badly enough about what has happened that we don't need to add to your misery," said David.

"I threw up again!" yelled Dylan from his bedroom. David hurried from the room.

"I'd like to make lunches with you for a while, Hailey. We can decide together what you can eat. And, if you get up a half hour earlier, then you should always have time for breakfast," added Alexandra. "Does that sound like a plan?"

"Definitely." Hailey grinned. She was relieved she wasn't in as much trouble as she had feared. Maybe things would work out after all.

Chapter Fourteen

Hailey woke up early the morning of the Science Centre trip. She yawned and pulled the covers up more securely around her; she would just lie there for five more minutes. She could not believe how fast the last six weeks had gone. Having Samantha and Julie at school made everything so much better and a lot of fun; some days she had to use her puffer frequently because of all the laughing she did! She was doing well in all her classes, too. As Hailey pulled her feet out from under the covers, an interesting thought occurred to her: maybe it was because she was having so much fun that she was getting such good grades.

Hailey was also happy the trip meant she would miss Gym. Even though Simms was aware of her asthma and didn't push her as hard, Hailey was never going to like Gym class, or Mrs. Simms.

When Hailey heard Dylan bumping around in his room, she decided it was time to get up.

She ambled into the kitchen and saw Dylan was still in his pyjamas, clutching his book about airplanes.

"Good morning, Dylan," she said, edging past him on her way to sit at the table.

"Hi, Hailey," answered Dylan.

He turned to Alexandra. "Did you throw all the purple ones away?" Dylan asked Alexandra as he gestured toward the large bowl of candy on the counter.

"Yes, I did." Alexandra tousled his hair and brought the treat bowl down for him to inspect.

"I not like trick or treating anymore," he declared.

The night before had been Halloween and they had gone trick or treating. When they got home, Dylan had stuffed a purple gobstopper in his mouth and seconds later, he had started choking. Hailey would not forget the look in his eyes as he struggled to draw air into his blocked airway.

Alexandra had quickly stepped behind him and helped him spit the candy out. She had explained later that the first aid technique she had used was known as abdominal thrusts. Hailey was relieved Alexandra had the situation under control and shuddered to think what would have happened if Dylan had choked at the Dunlops'!

David came into the kitchen.

"Psst, Dylan, over here." He whispered something in Dylan's ear and slipped something behind his back.

Dylan skipped over to Hailey and handed her what David had passed him from behind his back. It was a brightly wrapped package. "Surprise!" shouted Dylan. "It's for you. Open it."

Hailey unwrapped the package. Inside was a beautiful blue sweater.

"I made it myself," said Alexandra. "Why don't you try it on?"

Hailey put the sweater on. It felt soft against her skin and was warm. "Thanks for the sweater," she grinned. Hailey was touched that Alexandra made her a homemade gift. Alexandra had put a lot of thought and effort into it.

"Look closely at the front inside of it," urged David.

Hailey looked down and found a small zippered pocket. "Hey, cool!" she exclaimed.

"We thought you could put your inhaler in that pocket and keep it safe and secure there," added Alexandra.

"That's great," said Hailey. "You guys think of everything."

"Do you like it?" asked Dylan as he hopped up and down.

"I love it," replied Hailey. "I'm going to wear it to school."

Once Hailey arrived at school, everyone was divided into smaller groups for the trip. Hailey was in a group with Samantha and Julie.

On the bus, Mr. Hetherington began taking attendance and giving last minute instructions. "Stay with your group and don't run everywhere," he commanded. "After the morning workshops, you'll have the whole afternoon to look at whatever you want to," reminded the math teacher.

Hailey sat back in her seat and pressed her hand to her side. Yes, her inhaler was still there, safely zipped up.

Once they arrived at the Science Centre, the morning workshops on electricity and voice-activated computer programs couldn't go by quickly enough. Hailey wanted to see as much as she could. She wondered if the demonstrator would ever stop droning on.

Finally, it was lunchtime. "Wouldn't it be great if we could see a movie at the IMAX theatre?" sighed

Julie as she dipped her french fry into some ketchup. The girls were sitting in the large cafeteria on the main level of the Science Centre.

Hailey nodded as she opened her lunch bag. Samantha and Julie immediately leaned over and peered into her bag. "What note did your mom give you today?" they asked.

Hailey laughed. "Give me a minute to get it out and read it." She pulled the note out and unfolded it. "It's a joke: how many teenagers does it take to screw in a light bulb? Only one, but she'll spend two hours on the phone talking about it."

"Hahaha!" guffawed the girls.

Ever since Alexandra and Hailey had been making lunches together, Alexandra had started putting little heart-shaped notes in her lunch every day. It was always exciting to open her lunch and read that day's note, but sometimes it seemed like Samantha and Julie were more excited about her notes than she was!

"If we hurry, we can go to that science arcade the demonstrator was talking about," suggested Hailey.

Although Mr. Hetherington had warned against running, Hailey, Samantha, and Julie couldn't help but run from display to display; it was so amazing touching everything and playing the games. Every now and then

Hailey patted her pocket to make sure the inhaler was there. With all the running, talking, and laughing she was doing, she would need it again soon.

"Let's go to the electricity display," suggested Julie.

"The demonstrators get someone to put their hand on this giant ball and all their hair stands up," added Samantha. "It works really well with long hair."

Hailey tugged on Samantha's long, blond hair. "You just want to be chosen to put your hand on that ball," she teased.

Julie looked at her program. "It starts in ten minutes. We better head over there."

Most of the other students appeared to have the same idea, and it became crowded and hot around the silver ball. Hailey could feel the sweat drip down her back. She took off her sweater and tied it around her waist. After the demonstration, the three girls went to look at the IMAX theatre.

"Look, they're playing *Jurassic Park*!" exclaimed Samantha. "Can you imagine those dinosaurs on that huge screen? It would be like you're right in the movie!"

"Too bad we have to leave soon," said Julie. "Maybe I'll get my parents to take me here on the weekend."

Hailey only nodded. The last run to the theatre had made her chest feel really tight. "I'm going to the washroom," she said. "I'll be right back."

Hailey slipped into the nearby washroom, went into a stall, and untied her sweater. She reached into the pocket, but couldn't find her inhaler. She knew she had used her inhaler before lunch. Suddenly, she couldn't remember if she had zipped up the pocket. Hailey felt her heart sink—she had to find the inhaler, she just had to! If she didn't find it, she knew the snowboarding trip would be cancelled.

Hailey hurried out of the washroom. "I lost something," she said quickly. "I have to find it. I'll meet you guys at the front when we have to leave," she added. She took off so quickly she didn't give her friends time to answer.

First Hailey headed for the electricity display. She had taken off her sweater there; maybe that's where her inhaler was. But where was the display? Hailey had followed Julie and Samantha without paying attention to where they were going.

After ten minutes of walking around in circles, she found an employee of the Science Centre and asked her for directions to the display. As soon as she found it, she scanned the area. Hailey's hands were shaking and her legs felt like Jell-O. What if she didn't find her inhaler? Her wheezing was getting louder and it was getting harder to get air in; she knew she'd have to go to the hospital if she didn't find it soon. What would the Marcottes say when she told them she lost her inhaler again? Alexandra had even made her a special sweater to keep it safe! Hailey knew there would be no trip if she didn't find it, and maybe, no adoption!

Just then, Hailey spotted her inhaler lying beside the steps leading up to the silver ball. As she rushed toward the steps, an employee of the centre was coming down them, staggering under the weight of a large box he was carrying. Hailey saw the box start to shift in his arms. As the heavyset employee adjusted his stance to catch the falling box, he stepped right on her inhaler, crushing it!

Chapter Fifteen

Hailey charged forward. "Hey, you stepped on my inhaler!" she wheezed. The young man quickly moved his foot and she dove for her inhaler. But, as she picked it up, Hailey realized there was no way she was getting a puff out of it—it was completely squashed. She sank down on the steps. She needed to get her breathing under control. Hailey put her head down and took several deep, slow breaths.

When Hailey was breathing more normally, she looked at her watch. She had to head back or she would miss attendance. She walked slowly to the entrance of the Science Centre where Mr. Hetherington spotted her. "We were just going to send out a search party for you," he scolded. "Let's go. On the bus, everyone."

Hailey spent the bus trip back to school trying to decide what to do. Was there a way she could replace the inhaler without the Marcottes knowing? But how? When? If only she hadn't lost it! There was no way the Marcottes would want to adopt her now; they were better off with just Dylan.

Suddenly, Julie poked her. "Hey space cadet, we're here."

Hailey picked up her backpack and got off the bus, her thoughts a wild jumble in her head. She couldn't face David right now. How could she go back and live with them? Hailey jammed her hands in her pockets and started walking. Walking had always made her feel better.

Without even realizing it, she made her way to the park near the Marcottes' house. Hailey sank down onto a bench and dropped her backpack with a thud near her feet.

She looked up at the sound of excited chatter. A little girl and her mother had come into the park. Hailey watched the girl happily swinging off the monkey bars and going down the slide. She wished she could feel as happy and carefree again as that little girl did.

Hailey scuffed her feet on the dirt as she blinked away hot tears. It had all been too good to last. She thought about what a nuisance she had been, right from the start. If she wasn't using her hands as napkins, she was getting lost on the ferry or giving attitude about a simple trip to the park. It would have been her fault if Dylan had taken some puffs of the inhaler she had carelessly misplaced and gotten sick. She'd made them worry when she fainted in the lunch room and Alexandra had missed half a day of work because of that. She'd been rude during family meetings and downright nasty about the new clothes they had bought her. She might as well have carried around a sign saying, "don't adopt me; I'm trouble." The Marcottes had been nothing but nice to her and that was how she repaid them!

A loud cry interrupted her musings. Hailey looked over at the playground equipment: the little girl had fallen from the structure, scraping her knees.

"I'm sorry, Mommy," cried the little girl. "I ripped the new pants you bought me."

Hailey was surprised to hear the girl's mother laugh in response. "Oh honey, pants can be replaced. I'm more worried about you and your knees. Let's get you cleaned up. I think I still have a Band-Aid or two."

Hailey stretched out her legs in front of her and thought about what to do. Would the Dunlops take her back—even for a short while? Maybe she could go live with Keisha's aunt?

She suddenly became aware of a ringing sound coming from her backpack. It was sure to be David calling, wondering where she was. When she opened her bag to hit ignore on her phone, her squashed inhaler fell out. The sight of that stupid inhaler made her so angry! Hailey picked it up and threw it into the woods as hard as she could; she wanted that busted inhaler as far away from her as possible!

But even after she'd thrown it, she could still see it on the ground in the forest. Fuelled by the rage bubbling up inside her, Hailey stood up, stomped over to the inhaler, and threw it again. This time it went a little further, but still not far enough. One more throw would do it.

Hailey ran over, picked it up, threw it again, then walked over to it and stomped on it—over, and over, and over, until she could hardly breathe and sweat was trickling down her back.

Her rage now dissipated, Hailey sank down on the forest floor, which was covered with a thin layer of fallen evergreen needles. As she idly ran her fingers through the needles, she became aware of the sound of crunching leaves and twigs. She looked up and saw a coyote standing not thirty feet away!

Hailey froze. It was so quiet she became aware of another sound that reminded her of little puppies yipping as they played. She turned in the direction of the sound and saw—just off the path she was sitting on—two young coyotes! They were partially hidden in a pile of branches.

Had Hailey been in a better mood that day they all went to the park, she might have paid better attention to what David had been saying about coyotes. They were like dogs, she remembered. Dogs, she knew from personal experience, liked to chase people when they ran. Would the coyotes think it was a game and chase her if she ran? Hailey suspected the mother coyote wouldn't think it was a game, though. She would want to protect her babies from danger.

Hailey knew she had to get out of there, quickly and quietly, without making the mother think she was going to hurt her pups. Running was not an option; Hailey was already struggling to breathe properly.

Hailey stood up carefully and walked backwards slowly. Every step felt like it took an eternity. The coyote hadn't moved, and Hailey made sure every step she took was away from where the young coyotes were playing. Just as she figured she must be nearing the edge of the forest, Hailey stumbled and fell over a large tree branch—she went sprawling and the coyote lunged forward!

Hailey got up and ran as fast as she could toward the park, her heart pounding fast and hard. She made it to the bench and collapsed onto it, wheezing and coughing uncontrollably. The coyote could eat her for all she cared. Nothing mattered now but desperately trying to inhale as deeply as she could to get any amount of air into her lungs.

Hailey was just starting to see spots at the edges of her vision when David ran up to her. All his hair was standing straight up, as if he had been running his hands through it constantly. His face was red and it reminded her of how she looked when she was fighting back tears.

"We're getting you to the hospital right now," David said once he had assessed the situation. He picked her up, and moments later, they were in the car. "Alexandra's there and she will help get your asthma attack under control."

Hailey leaned back against the seat of the car. As she struggled for breath, the words of the mother in the park came back to her. Hailey now understood why the mother had laughed. Pants, inhalers—all that could be replaced. A parent's primary concern was for the health and safety of their children because children could not be replaced.

At the hospital, Hailey was quickly taken care of. Alexandra was right there, giving her an oxygen mask and making sure she took two puffs of an inhaler. Alexandra and David never left her side.

When Hailey could breathe comfortably again, she had so many questions.

"Where's Dylan?" she asked first.

"Once I realized you were missing, I asked if he could stay at a friend's house. He's there now and doesn't realize what's happened. He just thinks it's a playdate," explained David.

"How did you know where to find me?"

"You left your phone and your backpack by the bench at the entrance to the woods. I kept calling your phone and the constant ringing alerted a parent who was at the park with her little girl. She picked it up and answered it, letting me know where you were."

"What about the coyote?"

"The coyote went back into the woods. Once it reached the edge of the park, it turned and left."

"Wow, you think of everything," was all Hailey could say as she fidgeted with the tube on her oxygen mask.

Later that evening, Hailey, David, and Alexandra picked up Dylan from his friend's and went home. Hailey was glad to let David and Alexandra tuck Dylan into bed; she was exhausted. After a long, hot shower, she crawled into her bed. Never had Hailey been so glad to be safely in bed!

David and Alexandra came into her room.

"We were wondering if you feel like talking about what happened today," said Alexandra as she sat down on the edge of the bed.

Many things had become clear to Hailey that afternoon. She'd had a lot of time to think while she lay in the hospital bed.

"I don't mind telling you what happened," said Hailey. It would feel so good to get everything off her chest. "The Science Centre trip was great, right up until someone accidentally stepped on my inhaler and busted it," began Hailey. "You made me that special sweater to keep my inhaler safe and I still lost it. I didn't think I could face coming home and telling you about it. I was scared you wouldn't want to adopt me anymore because I didn't take care of my inhaler, and I figured when you said you would cancel the snowboarding trip, what you really meant was you wouldn't adopt me after all."

"Oh Hailey," interrupted Alexandra. "That is so wrong! We were overly harsh in threatening to cancel the trip, but that never meant we wouldn't adopt you!

We love you so much." Alexandra broke off and reached for a tissue to wipe away tears.

David cleared his throat. "There is nothing you can do that would make us change our minds about adopting you; you're stuck with us for a very long time. We can hardly wait to adopt both of you, no matter what."

Hailey sat up and enveloped David and Alexandra in a long, long, hug. "I know now how much you love me, and that you would never give up on me. I'm just sorry I had to end up in the hospital and scare you before I could figure that out."

"You do do things in a big way," laughed Alexandra.

Hailey couldn't help but join in on Alexandra's laughter, and soon David was laughing too. Hailey hadn't felt so good in a very long time.

Dylan appeared at the door to Hailey's room, rubbing his eyes. "What's so funny?" he wanted to know. "You woke me up."

As she jumped out of bed and gave him a monster hug, Hailey said, "Sorry we woke you up Dyl-Pickle, we're just happy to be a family."

Chapter Sixteen

The next two weeks seemed to fly by. Hailey stood at her window and savoured the last candy bar from her Halloween stash; she had allotted one candy for each day from Halloween until today: Adoption Day. As she gazed out the window, she smiled as she watched David and Dylan raking leaves. Well, David was raking and Dylan was doing his best to flatten every pile of leaves he could find.

Hailey turned from the window as Alexandra came into her room. "Are you nervous?" Alexandra asked.

"No, I just hope Dylan doesn't have a seizure while we're talking with the judge," Hailey mused. He wasn't sick, but Hailey was so wound up and excited about today, she couldn't stop herself from fretting about any possible thing going wrong, no matter how unrealistic.

Alexandra shrugged. "If he does, we'll just handle it like we always do."

"Yeah, that's true," answered Hailey. Dylan's last seizure had been over a month ago and Alexandra had handled it calmly and quickly.

"It's time to go," said Alexandra. "It's pretty cold today; please put on your new jacket."

Hailey played with the zipper on her jacket the entire ride to the courthouse. *What if the judge decided they wouldn't make a good family? What if Dylan told the judge he thought David was mean because he'd been sent to time-out two days in a row? What if the judge decided the Marcottes were too strict and shouldn't be parents after all? What if the pen ran out of ink?!*

Hailey was so lost in thought it wasn't until David tapped her on the shoulder that she realized they were already at the door to the judge's chambers. She noticed the Dunlops were there as well; they both rushed over to smother her and Dylan with hugs.

Once they were all in and seated, Dylan climbed onto Alexandra's lap. He turned to Alexandra and whispered loudly, "Are we going to talk to God now?"

Everyone laughed, including the judge. "Why do you think I'm God?" he asked.

Dylan cuddled closer to Alexandra. "I was looking at a book yesterday and God had on a long black shirt, just like you."

"I see," responded the judge solemnly. "Well, I'm not God; this long robe is to let everyone know I am a judge. You don't have anything to be afraid of, Dylan."

Hailey was so happy to have a brother like Dylan. With one simple question, he had diffused the stress and tension and now everyone could relax.

The judge shuffled some papers on his desk. "Hailey, what is your favourite part of being in the Marcotte family?" he asked.

Hailey smiled. That was an easy question! "It's great to be able to relax and be a kid, and not have to worry so much about my brother. I know Alexandra and David do an excellent job taking care of him and his seizures. I never thought I'd trust anyone enough to share the responsibility of looking after my little Dyl-Pickle," she answered proudly.

Everyone laughed, including Dylan.

The judge then smiled at Dylan. "Well, Mr. Dylan, what do you like best about being a Marcotte?"

Dylan hugged Alexandra and then he leaned over and hugged David. He hopped off Alexandra's lap, ran over, and hugged Hailey. "I like having a mommy and a daddy who give lots of hugs and who love me lots and don't get scared when I fall down and have the shakes."

The judge smiled. "That is one of the best answers I have heard in a long time."

"Can I say one more thing?" asked Dylan.

"Of course," chuckled the judge.

"I like it that Hailey smiles lots more now, and she has more fun with me 'cause she's just my big sister and not a mommy."

"That was well put, Dylan," complimented the judge. "I have heard all I need to from you to feel very comfortable in helping you all become a family. Let's sign those papers!"

Epilogue

Five weeks later in British Columbia...

"That airplane ride was so fun," exclaimed Dylan as he sat on the floor pulling on his snow pants. Hailey smiled over at her brother; the plane ride had been fantastic. They had been at the resort since the day before, and Dylan still could not stop talking about the plane ride. He was already anticipating the plane ride home.

Hailey squatted over her suitcase as she looked through it for her favourite blue sweater. Her whole body ached. She had spent most of the day before on the bunny slopes, learning how to ride the snowboard. She had fallen and gotten up at least fifty times, but now she had mastered the basic skills. Today she was going to try out the smallest of the medium-sized hills.

"Boo!" shouted Dylan, tiptoeing up behind her. "Ooh, you're gonna be in trouble," he crowed.

"Hey, don't sneak up on me like that," shouted Hailey. Dylan had seen that she had brought along the special Christmas gift given to her by David and Alexandra. It was the tattered photo of her, Dylan, and their parents. The Marcottes had put it in a beautiful frame for her, and Alexandra had expressly told her not to bring it in case it got broken or lost.

At that moment, Alexandra walked into their room. "What's going on here?"

Hailey quickly shoved the photo to the bottom of her suitcase.

"Hailey Williams-Marcotte, what are you hiding from me?" Alexandra asked sternly.

"I know you said I shouldn't bring it, but I just had to have the photo along for our trip. I need to look at the picture every day," Hailey answered sheepishly. "Sometimes I worry I'll forget what my parents looked like."

Alexandra gave Hailey a hug. "You can always talk to me, Hailey. I'm disappointed you went behind my back and brought the photo despite what I said, but I understand. You wouldn't have had to deceive me if you had just talked with me and explained your feelings."

Hailey nodded. It was still hard for her to confide in David and Alexandra. Three years in the foster care system had made her very independent and self-reliant; it was a daily struggle for her to open up and share her feelings. It helped enormously, though, that Alexandra and David had an endless supply of love and patience for her and Dylan.

"When you're done hugging, can we go sliding, Mommy?" asked Dylan.

"Yes," laughed Alexandra. "Let's see how fast you can finish getting into your snowsuit," she challenged him.

"Oh, and Hailey, be sure to take two puffs before we head out," Alexandra reminded her.

"I'm way ahead of you, Mom," announced Hailey smugly.

Hailey grinned to herself. In just a few minutes, she would be strapping her new, freshly waxed snowboard on. She would be getting off the chair lift for her first trip down the hill. She could almost feel the wind on her face and the snow spraying all around her! Maybe one day she would have a chance to be in the Olympics and carve her own path to greatness, just like her idol! It felt great to be a kid in the Marcotte family—anything was possible.